D1366498

Speak No Evil

BY MIGNON G. EBERHART

IN THIS FASCINATING NOVEL, destiny carries several people to their deaths and several others to the shadow of the gallows. Critics have often commented on the high quality of Mrs. Eberhart's character drawing, and her uncanny skill in creating eerie suspense, but she has outdone herself in this book. The events take place in and about a villa on an estate at Montego Bay on the beautiful tropical island of Jamaica. The author makes full use of the colorful background, the velvety black nights and the occasional fogs drifting in from the bay to throw a pall over creeping terror and deeds of violence.

Against this scene unfolds the story of Elizabeth Dakin, who is married to a millionaire dipsomaniac, and who is preparing her escape when he is shot. Suspicion immediately falls on her, but there are others in the tangled affairs of the Dakin household: Dyke Sanderson, Dakin's nephew, with whom Elizabeth had once had a fleeting romance; Cyril Kirby, the English yachtsman who clearly understands and sympathizes with Elizabeth's unhappiness; Dakin's first wife, who arrives to safeguard her share of the estate; and Ruth Reddington—cool, audacious, efficient business associate of Dakin, who bluntly tells Inspector Friker that Elizabeth is the only one who could have committed the murder.

Then there is the little lucky piece of three monkeys with the motto, "Hear no evil, speak no evil, see no evil," which was there on the table beside the dead man and which so mysteriously disappeared.

This is more than a mystery story. It is a novel of great emotional intensity and Mrs. Eberhart's best to date.

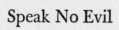

Speak No Evil

Books by Mignon G. Eberhart

Speak No Evil

BY MIGNON G. EBERHART

Random House · New York

FIRST PRINTING

Speak No Evil

All the persons and events in this book are entirely imaginary. Nothing in it derives from anything which ever happened.

THE AUTHOR

I

THE BRUTAL and cold-blooded murder of Robert Dakin was actually a thing of slow growth, with roots that, like a noxious plant, spread slowly over a period of years.

But to Elizabeth Dakin, his young wife, it was sudden and unforecast. She had often been afraid of him; never for him.

Yet even the events immediately leading up to that tragedy moved with a certain inevitability and momentum as if once started they could not be stopped.

The letter from Dyke was the first one.

"My darling," began the letter, "don't go to your lawyers yet. Give him and yourself and me a little more time."

Elizabeth, reading it, thought back over the past two years which seemed endless. Time? She held the letter under the light, for it was already dusk in her bedroom.

"It seems such a short time since we were all at

St. Moritz; it seems, now, absurd that such a trivial thing could have separated us. But the next thing I knew you were married to him. Elizabeth, I want you to wait—and do nothing and say nothing for a little longer. I haven't changed at all during the two years since I've seen you. Thank you for writing to me as you did, but hold on a little longer. Your letter— forgive me, darling—was a little hysterical. This is hurried; I'll write more later. All my love." It was signed Dyke and below it was a postscript.

"Better destroy this; it wouldn't do for Uncle Bob to get hold of it."

She read the letter slowly again. It had come, forwarded from England, in the afternoon post, almost six weeks to the day after she had written—at last, after two years—to Dyke. She put the letter in the pocket of her gray silk slacks and went through the open French doors out onto the balcony.

It was that chill and quiet hour in the tropics when the sun drops out of sight and the sea turns purple. Elizabeth went to the vine-hung balustrade and leaned upon it, her chin in her hands. The long, sprawling villa lay amid its gardens and royal palms and yellow stone walls on one of the hills above Montego Bay. So from the balcony there was a wide encircling view of the old flat little town of Montego Bay, with its white and pink stucco and its gray stone blent companionably together, and of the deep curve of the bay and the small Bogue Islands set like dark emeralds within its cup, and, beyond, the endless

4

reach of sea and sky. Golden and dappled under the sun, at dusk the sea, the Spanish Main, turned purple and somber and mysterious, withdrawing itself into the purple twilight.

The waves washed rhythmically against the dim line of coast away below and Elizabeth listened and thought of the letter she had just received, and of the letter she had written, to which Dyke's letter was a reply. He had said it was hysterical, and perhaps it was; for it had been written in a moment of something like terror—a queer feeling that leaped all at once from that deep lurking sense of apprehension that, lately, had grown so familiar to her. It had been a frantic, hurried little letter. She could scarcely remember the scrawled phrases, except that she had told Dyke that her marriage had to end; that there was nothing she could do for Robert and nothing he would do for himself; that it had all been a horrible mistake for which she had paid dearly.

Dyke's reply had been written, as he said, hurriedly. But he had said definitely that he hadn't changed. That meant—didn't it?—in any way.

A lemon-colored star came out and shone above the purple sea, and she looked at it, thinking.

Her marriage to Major Robert Dakin, a man twenty-five years her senior and a confirmed dipsomaniac (she hadn't, naturally, known that at the time of their marriage; she thought now of her childish credulousness with astonishment), had been a marriage of heartbreak and of horror. She wondered

5

just when during those two years, remembering Dyke's gaiety and youth like a picture, the clearer and finer for the time and distance between them, she had fallen in love with him. She must have fallen in love with him, for otherwise she wouldn't have turned to him, in her trouble, and asked his help.

Dyke. She tried to summon his face against the clear twilight sky—his smile, his warm dark eyes, the lean curve of his cheek—and, for the first time in those months, failed altogether.

There was a sound from the room beyond the open French doors, her bedroom. Robert? She turned, swiftly and warily. On guard.

When she actually faced Robert, when she appeared in public with him, she was able to conceal that wariness; she was able to uphold the position she had adopted, defensively and instinctively, from the first, and it was that of a loved and respected wife.

She wondered briefly now—listening for sounds from her bedroom—whether those closest to them did not, now and then, see through that thin and perilous mask. Charlie Hawes, for instance; he was Robert's secretary. He lived in the house or traveled with them. He couldn't have helped seeing and knowing too much. He knew about Robert.

And then she thought suddenly: Charlie's afraid, too. She realized she had known that for a long time. It was in his pale, wistful face; it was in the way his narrow shoulders shrank together when Robert shouted at him; it was in the nervous way he ran here

6

and there, quickly, hurrying to do Robert's slightest bidding. Yes. Charlie felt as she did. Particularly since they had come to Jamaica unexpectedly and hurriedly a month ago from England. For the duration of the war, Robert had said, and had pulled every string he knew to get passage for the whole household. He'd owned the house in Jamaica for years, along with an interest in a sugar estate. It was not strange to him as it was to Elizabeth—strange and big and lonely with the servants shut away in their own wing, leaving herself and Charlie to deal with Robert.

She took a long breath. And Robert shouted suddenly and peremptorily from inside the bedroom, "Elizabeth! Elizabeth!"

In spite of herself she hurried to the French doors. In spite of herself she replied quickly, "Yes, Robert. What is it? Here I am." And heard the placative, anxious note in her voice with something like horror; it was so like Charlie Hawes'.

Robert Dakin stood in the middle of the room; towering there, staring at her vaguely yet angrily. He was a big man, big-boned and heavy with still powerful muscles under the sagging flesh. He had a jutting, formidable chin, a sharply aquiline nose and bloodshot, nervous blue eyes. He had once been handsome and well set up; even now, dressed for the evening, pulling himself together for an hour or two, he was attractive—urbane, pleasant, self-possessed. If the dinner or bridge didn't last too long.

Two years ago, when she married him, that was the only side of him she had seen.

She watched him now, anxiously.

He didn't speak for a moment but stood there, his hands in the pockets of his thin silk dressing gown, rocking slightly on his feet and frowning at her with black eyebrows which, like his gray-streaked hair, were thick and heavy. Then he passed a hand across his unsteady, purplish mouth, took something from his pocket and came toward her. She tried not to shrink from the unsteady bulk of him, advancing toward her.

"I've got something pretty for you," he said. "You've never worn them before." He dropped a handful of jewels on the table beside her as carelessly as if they had been marbles.

"Charmian's," he said, and chuckled.

She looked at them and caught her breath. "But these—these are magnificent," she said.

"Sure they are. It took her years to collect them." He chuckled again. "Take a look at the necklace."

"But I . . ."

"Look at it. Take it in your fingers. I'm not going to tell you what I paid for that. Like it, do you?"

Because he thrust it at her, she held the thing in her fingers. Its magnificence almost shocked her; there were emeralds (not matched but alike) set intricately with diamonds that were literally like drops of dew.

"It's—beautiful."

8

"Here, give it to me."

He took it from her fingers, pushed her tailored yellow blouse away from her throat and placed the necklace around her neck. His fingers fumbled unsteadily with the fastening.

"Let me . . ." she said, but he brushed her hands away.

"No. There . . ." He put heavy hands on her shoulders and turned her to face him.

In the mirror across the room she caught the incredible glow of green from the emeralds, the glitter of perfect diamonds against her white skin. It was absurdly incongruous above her simple gray slacks and yellow blouse. Incongruous and a little frightening in some obscure way as if the cold jewels had some secret and inimical life of their own. She reached up to unfasten and remove the necklace, but he caught her hands.

"No. They suit you. You'll wear 'em tonight."

"Tonight?"

"Certainly. How Charmian liked those emeralds! She was determined to take them with her when she left me, you know. I stopped her. She had them in her handbag. I took them away from her. Sure, you're to wear them. You're my wife, aren't you?"

"But—tonight?"

"Why not tonight?"

"It—it isn't suitable. To dinner with Cyril? To the hotel later? Robert, I can't wear them tonight. People don't . . ."

9

"You'll wear 'em, if I say so." He pushed his hands in his pockets and rocked a little again. She saw then that he was very pale; it was a queer chalky pallor that she recognized. "Very well. I'll wear them."

"Good girl." He patted her shoulder. "Wear white satin. Nothing so becoming to emeralds as white satin—white, bare skin. Good girl." He patted her chin, too, fumblingly, turned and walked to the door.

A bad attack was coming, then. She had not been mistaken. Those first small symptoms which now she could recognize had warned her. The first irritability, the first restlessness, the first slight unexpectedness of conduct which was not quite eccentricity.

But at the door he turned. "Oh, by the way," he said, "Dyke is coming."

"Dyke!"

"Gets here tomorrow on the *Baragua*. Tomorrow at noon at Kingston."

After a moment she said the only thing that came to her lips. "Why didn't you tell me he was coming?"

Major Dakin blinked and smiled. "Didn't think of it," he said. He turned fumblingly and went back along the passage to his study.

There was presently the sharp tinkle of ice in a glass from the study and a murmur of voices. Charlie was there with him—or Leech, the white-haired, kind old butler, used to Robert and his ways.

At last she took out Dyke's letter again. It was dated over a month earlier. Her letter to him had gone by air; his reply had been sent to England just

10

before they had left England and before the news of their departure and destination had been cabled to him by Robert. It had been opened by censor; she touched the printed label absently with her finger. That and the confusion in shipping since the war had further delayed it. She read the letter once more slowly.

This time, when she tried, she could see his face clearly in her mind. Smiling at her gaily, reassuringly. Telling her he still loved her. Telling her to wait and trust him. Not, of course, that his letter had said just that. But he was coming.

2

FINALLY the small quick tick of the clock that stood on the desk roused her. They were to dine that night with Cyril Kirby, on his yacht, and later to appear at the war benefit at the hotel; she must dress.

There was no fireplace in the house—or in all Jamaica so far as she knew. She touched a match to Dyke's letter and put it in an ashtray and, leaning upon the table, watched it burn.

A long mirror opposite reflected her: red-gold hair, rolled smoothly over her small head, white and rather clear profile, gray eyes deeply shadowed by dark eyelashes, crimson mouth a little sad. Her face had decision and temperament and, in moments of happiness, a certain luminous beauty. It was, now, withdrawn and thoughtful against the pale green walls of the very cool, very spacious bedroom, with its jalousied windows; its great mahogany bed draped in mosquito netting; its long, low bookshelves. It was a room she would have liked had it not been in Robert's house, adjoining (by way of a small passage leading between her bathroom on one side and her dressing room on the other) Robert's own suite.

When the note was fully consumed, she went to the bell, rang it, and waited for her maid. Presently there were voices, one light and feminine, from Major Dakin's study and a quickly stilled giggle. Marianna, of course; she always giggled when the Major hurled a not-too-subtle pleasantry her way. This time it sounded as if the pleasantry had not been a spoken one. To reach Elizabeth's suite, it was necessary to pass through Major Dakin's big study and Marianna was never loathe to linger, if the opportunity offered. But in a moment the maid tripped lightly along the little passage. She was a little thing, smart in her black uniform with its white frilled apron and cap. It happened that she was the only servant in the house (all of them brought from the Devonshire place in England) who did not pre-date Elizabeth's marriage and who, therefore, had not been hired and trained by Charmian.

"Madame is ready to dress?"

"Yes. I'll wear the white satin. But first unfasten this catch for me, will you please?"

She could see the girl's face in the mirror behind her, dark, earnest, eyes alight with avid interest. "Madame, the emeralds! Yes, Madame. Ah, they are exquisite! One has heard of them. Naturally. In the kitchen. They belonged to . . ."

"Thank you, Marianna."

"Madame will be very beautiful," said Marianna and turned with a swish of silk and starch toward the bathroom.

Beautiful? thought Elizabeth. Young? Is that why he married me?

But she really did look as nearly beautiful as it was in her power to look when she was finally dressed in white satin that clung like a miracle to her breast and slender waist and fell in silvery folds to the floor. Her hair was dressed, now, high and fashionably, and the carefully arranged curls high on her head emphasized her Coolman look of race. She was too finely articulated and her features were too delicate ever to be imposing, but she did have an innate dignity and a good carriage.

"Thank you, Marianna." She picked up her little jeweled evening bag and gloves. "Go to bed whenever you like. Don't wait up for me. Good night."

She had reached the door, with Marianna following her and carrying the swirl of crimson chiffon flounces that was her long cloak, when they both remembered the emeralds and went back for them. Again the necklace felt cold and—which was absurd—slightly sinister upon her neck. The two rings were heavy on her fingers. The bracelet weighed down her wrist.

When she turned from the mirror Robert Dakin was standing again in the doorway. He, too, was dressed and ready to go. He looked cool and fresh in his white dinner jacket and he was in a fit of good humor, smiling approvingly. "Good," he said. He came forward, stopped to look at Elizabeth lingeringly and deliberately, and then reached out and pinched Marianna's ear before he took the wrap from the maid and put it around Elizabeth and kissed her shoulder as he did so.

As they passed through the wide hall on the lower floor, Charlie Hawes' pale face peered at them from the library doorway and instantly jerked out of sight. Leech, the butler, opened the door, eyes watching his master's face covertly and knowingly. Odd, that she'd had, now and then, an impression that he pitied her and would have helped her. Charlie reserved all his pity for himself.

The car was waiting with Armand, a little, hard-faced chauffeur, at the wheel. He, too, gave Robert Dakin a quick, anxious glance as he held the car door for their entrance. The whole household had been uneasy—instantly aware of that different uneasiness in Robert Dakin. The gravel crunched as they turned away from the entrance, and the long villa with its lighted windows and wide tiled and pillared steps loomed above them and then was gone.

It was not a long drive down to Montego Bay. Major Dakin, a big bulk in the corner of the seat with his white coat and shirtfront making a light spot in the gloom, slumped as he was likely to do into brooding silence. The road twisted through fields of sugar cane, black now with the throb of the motor rising above its rustle, down toward the sea. She looked out into the mysterious blackness of sea and sky and wondered where Dyke was now in that northern blackness, how near to Cuba—how near to Jamaica.

It was strange, after two years, to think of Dyke—so near.

After a while she tried to plan—there would be lawyers, arrangements, interviews. She could plan nothing.

Cyril's tiny motor launch was waiting for them. She held up her white satin skirt and the black water winked and glittered, reflecting lights from the launch, and from the riding lights of a few other yachts and motor boats. When they reached the small yacht Cyril himself was waiting for them at the top of the steps. He took both her hands and kissed her lightly.

"How splendid you are tonight! My God, what jewels! Hello there, Major."

"Hello, Cyril. Well, here we are, my boy. Here we are."

"Won't you come this way?"

He led them into the tiny salon.

Cocktails were waiting on the table. Cyril was, as always, a quiet but thoroughly gracious host, taking Elizabeth's wrap, seeing Robert Dakin was comfortably seated, pouring cocktails, ringing for more caviar.

He was the best of the few friends they had in Jamaica, and had come to Jamaica, as a matter of fact, on the same boat the Dakin household had taken from England. He was a blond, reticent, rather shy and very pleasant Englishman of about forty. He had been a soldier, which accounted perhaps for a rather fine-drawn look in his quiet and well-bred face. He had a very comfortable but not immoderate income from property he had inherited near Falmouth, a few miles from Montego Bay, and had come, hurriedly, on the outbreak of war, to see to that property and to sell his yacht before he was called up. He spent most of the year, however, in a cottage in Devonshire near the sea and near the house where Elizabeth and Robert Dakin had spent a part of that constantly uneasy, constantly traveling two years. It was their mutual interest in Jamaica, really, rather than the fact that they were neighbors, that brought him and Robert Dakin, and thus Elizabeth, into closer acquaintance and, at last, fairly intimate association. He was the typical Englishman of his class and kind; if that pleasant, almost gentle reserve covered a certain stubborn strength then it was seldom apparent. Probably he had been and would be again a very good soldier and officer.

It was a quiet dinner; the food was simple but perfectly cooked and served, the talk light and unforced. Robert, however, said little; the dinner was almost over when he mentioned Dyke.

"Dyke," he said, "is coming tomorrow. Arrives on the *Baragua*."

"Dyke?" said Cyril, lifting his sandy eyebrows.

"Oh, yes. Dyke Sanderson. That's your nephew, isn't it?"

"Cousin's son. Only relative I have, so far as I know. Nice boy; took my son's place, as a matter of fact, when he died; Dyke needs some hardship, hasn't had any. But he's all right. He'll develop."

"Boy? Isn't he in charge of your American oil interests?"

"Let me see; Dyke must be thirty or so. Older, of course, than my son would have been, if he had lived. He was eighteen when he died—six years ago. Drowned—didn't you know? Yes, Dyke is older. Old enough to be placed in charge. It's my organization, of course; he can't go very far wrong. I keep in touch with things."

Cyril said, "I've heard you mention him; it's been some time since he was here."

"Two years. He wouldn't be coming now, if it weren't for the helium."

"Helium?" There was no perceptible change in Cyril's face or in his eyes. His slender fingers peeling a peach did not hesitate or falter. Yet instantly there was something cold and bleak about him—intangibly he became, again, a soldier.

There was a marked pause before Robert Dakin answered. "M'm, yes. Of course it will be entirely under government lease."

"Naturally." Cyril paused, too, and then went on, "The helium-bearing gases must be in considerable quantity if they warrant helium production."

Robert Dakin moved restlessly. "Well, of course, all that is up to the Federal men back in the States. Dyke is only bringing me reports. There is no private production and sale of helium."

"Certainly a necessary restriction," said Cyril, suddenly pleasant and the host again. "Especially since the war." He glanced at Elizabeth. "Ready, my dear?" he said. "Suppose we all adjourn; Major and I can't sit here drinking with so lovely a lady waiting alone for us."

Robert Dakin, rising heavily in his chair, said, "Of course you understand, Cyril, that's confidential. About the helium, I mean."

"Naturally," said Cyril again. He pulled out Elizabeth's chair. "Shall we go to the hotel now or later?"

3

THEY WENT almost at once to the hotel. It was early, but the driving, tragic restlessness that possessed Robert Dakin would not have permitted their lingering long in the tiny salon. Elizabeth sensed it and Cyril must have seen it, too.

The long hotel was brightly lighted. The sea directly below reflected it glitteringly. It was full of people, of commotion, of talk; bridge tables were set up everywhere, several small roulette wheels were going, and in the bar rum punch was selling at five shillings a drink, for it was a war benefit and every possible effort was made to swell the fund. It was, in its lights, its gaily dressed women, in the stir and perfume and jewels, a miniature and tropical Monte Carlo. All the English colony were there and all the American colony and all the tourists whose purses were lavish. They chose roulette and she sat between them, watching; after a while she rose, strolled idly about the room and then into the gardens.

20

It was there that, sometime later, Cyril joined her. She was sitting on the balustrade above the sea, when he came strolling along the terrace.

"Elizabeth? I was looking for you."

She said in quick anxiety, "Robert?"

"Oh, no! No, he's all right. Playing. Seems to be enjoying it. Cigarette?" She took one and he lighted it for her and then sat, too, on the balustrade, looking out toward the sea. He said without any warning— harshly, as if it took him, too, by surprise, "Elizabeth, in God's name, why did you marry him?" Her hands tightened on the balustrade. And Cyril said, "Did you love him?"

There was a silence. She did not look at him, yet she was deeply aware of his presence beside her. And of the queer little surprise she felt when she heard herself reply, simply and honestly, "I didn't know love was so important."

"Then you—didn't love him?" His voice demanded truth.

"No, Cyril. But I meant to be a good wife to him. I've tried to be that . . ." Her throat tightened.

Cyril's hand came out through the dusk and touched her own hand lightly and then withdrew. "Why, then, did you marry him? There must have been a reason."

She put her hands together, clasping them tight. "There were three reasons," she said, still not looking at Cyril.

He put his cigarette to his lips, took it away again.

"Well," he said, "what were they?"

"My father's death," said Elizabeth. "And money—and another man."

"Sounds fairly comprehensive," he said, rather dryly. "Tell me more, Elizabeth. Don't mind telling me."

"I've thought of it—of everything—so much. It's—been a failure, you know."

"Go on, my dear."

It was easy to talk when he didn't watch her but just stood there at her side, looking out into the night, smoking quietly.

"It began, I think, with the money. I was the only child and my mother died many years ago, so if my father died all the Coolman money was to come to me. And—and everyone knew it. Consequently, there were . . ." she hesitated, and Cyril said,

"Fortune hunters. Naturally. But you're rather nice, you know, money or no money."

"I loved my father," she said. "And he loved me. We—we were together very much after I'd finished school. We traveled, we did everything we wanted to do. He was . . ." She stopped, and sheered away from the thoughts of the silent, shy man, so tender with her, so loving, so carefully guarding her from anything that might wound, who had been her father. "He died," she said abruptly, "quite suddenly. We were at St. Moritz. And Major Dakin was there. My father knew him—not very well, I believe. But Robert was everything that a girl would admire. A man

22

of the world, a man who'd made a tremendous success; he was respected, looked up to. You know how attractive he can be . . ."

"I know," said Cyril. "So you needed help and you turned to him."

"He was kind. I can't tell you how kind he was. He saw to everything. Lawyers came on from New York as soon as they could, but they were strange to me, impersonal. It was Robert who helped me about everything. Before I quite realized it, he had stepped into a place left so—so terribly vacant."

"And since he had so much money himself you were fairly certain he wasn't a fortune hunter," said Cyril.

"Yes. He seemed to me everything that was fine and I—I admired him and trusted him. More than—seeing him tonight—anyone could understand."

"I know," said Cyril again.

"Everything came at once. My father's death, all the responsibility of my inheritance, everything. We hadn't many real friends. My father wasn't the kind to make intimate friends; perhaps he'd been disillusioned, too."

"Too?"

"As I was. I was in the . . ." she tried to smile. "In the throes of one of the disillusionments when it all happened."

"Oh. The other man?"

"Yes." She thought of Dyke away off somewhere in that blackness, coming closer. "That was over two years ago. I—had reason to think he only wanted my

23

money—too; we quarreled and I sent him away. I was wrong. I realize now that I was wrong; but then before I could discover my mistake, things happened. Six weeks after my father's death I married Robert."

He tossed away the end of his cigarette.

"And how long after that did you know about his drinking?"

"Two months afterward. We were in the country—near your place." Her voice wavered. She wished she need never again remember it.

"Don't think of it," said Cyril, his own voice a little harsh.

"The first year I tried every way I could think of to make something of both our lives. To save him and—and myself. To keep the ideal of marriage I'd had when I married him. I—really, I tried, Cyril . . ."

Again his voice was harsh and unnatural. He said, "Yes, Elizabeth, I've watched you trying."

"But this past year . . ." She moved her hands hopelessly. "There's nothing I can do, Cyril. He's—past help. It's as if something inhuman had taken possession of him. It—it looks out of his eyes—it makes him say and do things . . ."

Cyril turned with a jerk toward her. "You oughtn't to have married him, you know. You oughtn't to have married anyone just then. Somebody ought to have stopped you. You were too shaken emotionally to know what you were doing; you needed a friend to stand by you; instead you took the refuge that was offered. I—I do understand, Elizabeth. But you've come to the end of it. You're going to leave him, you know."

"It isn't as easy as that, Cyril."

"There's nothing else to do. You can't right one wrong with another."

She might have told him, then, of her appeal to Dyke, but all at once, with alarm, she thought of Robert left alone. It was dangerous to leave him alone; you never knew.

"Oh, Cyril, I must go back to Robert. I must hurry."

There was a short silence. Then Cyril said, "All right. But don't be alarmed. He was playing quietly when I left him."

He put up his hands to assist her and she got down from the balustrade and then, standing so near him, she put her hands on his shoulders in a little gesture of gratitude. "Thanks, Cyril," she said. "You—always understand."

He put his arms around her and held her there, looking down at her through the dusk. "I do understand," he said. "But I meant what I said just now, Elizabeth. Sometime—soon, I'm going to talk to you again about it." He bent and kissed her cheek lightly, as he had done occasionally before, very gently. He lifted his head, still holding her.

And then suddenly and unexpectedly his arms tightened, holding her close to him, and he bent and kissed her mouth. It was a quick, hard kiss—as if to him, too, it was unexpected. He released her quickly, and said, a little unsteadily, "Shall we go?"

25

4

IN SILENCE they walked back to the brilliant lights of the hotel. It was a curious silence, with the mysterious black sky close above them and the sea whispering in the darkness below them, as it had done since the beginning of time.

Robert was still in his place at the table. She went to him and again watched the game for a while. Cyril, beside Robert, glanced at her once or twice in his usual friendly, quietly affectionate way. Robert, slouched low in his chair, eyes bloodshot and vague, did not look at her.

It was after midnight when she had the curious little encounter which was in itself so unimportant and was yet to have its bearing upon the events then on their way. She was in the women's lounge, seated before a mirror, putting lipstick on her mouth, touching her hair, when a woman sharing the long mirror said unexpectedly, "You must be Elizabeth."

Elizabeth turned with a little jerk. "But I—I'm sorry—I don't . . ."

"I am Charmian," said the woman, and smiled a little although her eyes were frankly curious.

Charmian, the first Mrs. Robert Dakin, was a woman of perhaps forty-five. She was extremely thin, with a lined, slender but rather intellectual face—a passionate face, too—on which emotions had left their mark in the deep lines around her mouth and around her large, deep-set eyes. Her reddish-brown hair was dry in texture but beautifully coiffed; her thin cheeks were touched with rouge; her sandy eyelashes were accentuated with black; her eyebrows carefully arched. Her mouth was wide and petulant, and too carefully made up. Her dress was exquisitely fresh and its mauve drapery was arranged about her shoulders and neck so as to conceal their thinness. But she looked wiry and full of restless energy. Not a happy woman, thought Elizabeth, although the extreme care spent on her appearance, the beauty of the jewels she wore, the bag she carried, the furs across her chair indicated a certain love for possessions. She received, Elizabeth knew, a staggeringly large alimony. And she was sophisticated, worldly—and tired.

Her great, heavy-lidded, green-gray eyes had fastened upon the emeralds at Elizabeth's throat and wrist. "I knew you were Elizabeth," she said with a kind of weary affability, "the moment I saw you. My emeralds, you know." Green fire glittered in the mirror. Charmian's eyes lingered on them and her eyelashes drooped a little. She said, "Do you wear them much?"

27

"The emeralds?" Elizabeth tried to keep an instinctive and immediate coolness out of her voice. "No. I—I didn't know you were here."

"Yes; I am staying in Montego Bay. I was in Paris when the war started; after so many years at the villa, you know, Jamaica is like home to me. So I came here as soon as I could. I leased a house in the hills for the winter. I'll go to New York in the spring. I'd heard you were here, of course; for the duration, I suppose— Bob always liked Jamaica. By the way, how is Bob?"

"He's about as usual."

"About as usual." Charmian lifted her penciled eyebrows. "That means he's drinking. Well, nobody can stop his drinking. If I had known how . . ." she let the implication rest. "It's like Bob to pick out a pretty wife. I must say I was surprised."

"Surprised?"

"That he'd married you," said Charmian. "I mean, you with all that money. He had enough money as it was. I suppose you were in love with him. Well, you can certainly have him, my dear. But I do think," said Charmian unexpectedly, "that I ought to have had the emeralds."

Elizabeth rose; she felt embarrassed and extremely uncomfortable and consequently became chill and over-dignified. She said, "I know nothing about it. Good-bye."

Charmian glanced at her, leaned nearer the mirror to scrutinize the line of her lips, and said, "Good-bye."

Another mirror faced Elizabeth as her silk skirt

28

swished gently toward the door. In it she saw both their reflections—the two Mrs. Dakins. Charmian had paused, lipstick in hand; again they looked at each other in a mirror and it was a mysterious look. There was almost a symbolism about seeing each other thus through facing mirrors. Up to then Charmian had existed to Elizabeth as a figure built up entirely of echoes of her, of things she had bought, done, said; of references to her which revealed only a small segment of her personality and character. Probably Elizabeth had been exactly that kind of shadowy figure to Charmian.

Elizabeth nodded to Charmian's reflection in the mirror and Charmian nodded back, as Elizabeth went out the swinging door. It was not until it had closed behind her that it occurred to her that Charmian's last look, caught unexpectedly there in the mirror, had not been at all friendly.

Robert and Cyril were waiting for her. Cyril had lost, he said, Robert had won.

"You've kept me waiting. I'm ready to go. Hurry up. The car's waiting." Robert was white and unsteady; his hands shook so that he dropped her coat and Cyril picked it up and put it gently around her.

The car was at the door and Robert, shaken with nervous impatience, hurried her into the tonneau. Cyril refused to let them drive him back to his waiting launch.

"I'll walk," he said, and took Elizabeth's hand. His face was sober and intent and he looked directly and deeply into Elizabeth's eyes. He said only, "Good night, Elizabeth. You'll let me know if . . ."

He stopped there. She said, understanding, "Thank you, Cyril. Good night." The car door was closed; he stood a moment on the steps watching them leave. She had a momentary glimpse of him, his arms raised in a gesture of farewell—a lean, soldierly figure outlined in black and white against the lights, with the breeze ruffling his sandy hair and a shadowy significance, somehow, in the stillness of his regard and his upraised hand. Then the car turned and she could no longer see him.

"What'd Cyril mean?" said Robert suddenly out of the shadow at her side.

"Cyril? Oh"—rather fantastically she told him the exact truth—"if I want him to come to the villa, I suppose."

"Oh. Yes, of course." There was silence in the shadowy tonneau of the car with the lights of the town flashing past the windows. They had passed through the town and turned along the dark road winding upward between sugar cane plantings when Major Dakin chuckled unexpectedly.

"He's rather taken with you, you know. Thinks I don't treat you right. Thinks I drink too much." The chuckle grew to an uproarious, horribly uncontrolled laugh.

She tried not to hear the laugh, but her hands were trembling. He leaned unsteadily toward her and said jerkily, "You look as if you hate me. You look as if you'd like to take a knife in your pretty hands and shove it in my heart."

"*Robert . . .*"

"Oh, I don't mind." He laughed again, until he gasped for breath. "I don't mind. It amuses me. You've hated me and you've been afraid of me since— for a long time now. Why don't you leave me?"

He was leaning very near her, pressing against her. He put his arm around her, drawing her closer to him and her wrap slipped back so the starched knife-like edge of his cuff pressed sharply into her soft shoulder. He was uncertain and fumbling in his movements and in the darkness of the tonneau that uncertainty, combined with his great shadowy bulk, was frightening. Was, again, terrifying.

Without warning, that deep, instinctive fear she had fought for so long rose to a peak; she could no longer control it. She shrank back against the cold glass of the window and cried, trembling, hearing her own words with a kind of horror; knowing it was the wrong time, the wrong place, yet unable to stop them, "I am going to leave you."

There was a short silence. He was perfectly still, as if her unexpected and unusual defiance had surprised him.

"I didn't mean to tell you—like this. But—our marriage has gone so wrong, Robert. Wrong for both of us."

He leaned forward and caught her shoulders savagely.

"Who's the man? If it's Cyril . . ."

"It isn't."

"It is Cyril! It's got to be. There's no other man you've been seeing."

"No, Robert, no. It isn't Cyril. You're wrong. I—I didn't mean . . ."

"Didn't mean to talk, is that it? You made a mistake. Why, by God, by the time I get through with him! I'll go to him tomorrow. No, tonight would be better. We'll go back . . ."

Actually he was hoisting himself forward as if to give an order to the chauffeur.

"No, no, you mustn't. It isn't Cyril." Her voice must have carried conviction. For there was another silence in the car—except for that heavy, difficult breathing. Then he said with the queerest deliberation:

"Then it's Dyke. Oh, Elizabeth, what a fool you are!"

She knew that. Had known it the instant she said words she could not retract. All at once he began to laugh again with that ugly effect of complete laxness.

"When I get through with Dyke he won't want you," he said. "Don't you realize that I'm his bankroll? He's not got a cent without me."

She was ashamed, tired, sad. She wished with all her heart she could undo what she had done. She turned to him and said soberly and sincerely, "Robert, let's not bicker about it. I'm sorry—I'm terribly

32

sorry. We've both made a mistake; can't we try together to undo that mistake? It's only fair . . ."

"You really are a fool. Surely, you know me better than to think I'll let you go to another man, and that man like a son to me. Do you think I want to be a laughingstock? You're my wife. And I won't let you go. So forget it."

"You can't stop me. There are laws."

"Determined, are you? Listen . . ." He stopped, as if merely to choose from many weapons. All his life he'd been powerful, a conqueror and a despot. He was so assured, so strong and powerful still, that she felt instantly certain that whatever weapon he chose he would be thoroughly able to wield to her destruction.

"Listen . . ." he went on at last. "If you try to leave me and go to Dyke, I'll smear you both over the front pages until no decent person will speak to you. I'll—I have money, I have influence and you are news. You're the Coolman heiress and every paper in the world has pictures of you, ready to use. I've given Dyke everything so far. He's never been able to stand on his own feet. Do you think he's going to want you after I've finished? Do you think . . ." He hesitated, and then said with the queerest, crafty note in his voice, "You're a civilized woman, Elizabeth; well, you're due for a shock. In a relationship like ours a man goes straight back to the primitive; don't put your faith in laws, Elizabeth. Before I let you go to Dyke, I'll strangle you with my own hands."

His hand hovered at her throat and at the emeralds around it. And then she saw over his great shoulder that the glass window between the tonneau and the driver's seat was down; the chauffeur had heard every word that was said. She hated herself, and for a moment she really did hate Robert Dakin. The whole unexpected scene was ugly and violent, and incredible—and it was happening.

She said, low, "Robert, the window—Armand."

He, too, had had a moment in which to collect himself. His hands dropped away from her throat. He did not roll up the glass so Armand could hear no more. But he said almost quietly that they would talk later.

And he sat there beside her, clasping her with an arm that was still strong and powerful. His great physical strength presented one of the problems of his periodic drinking bouts. Certainly he couldn't have endured prolonged physical exertion; but there were moments, all too frequent, when nothing was safe from the violence of his sudden, unreasonable rages. It was why Charlie Hawes was so afraid of him.

Violence. It was the one essential word in describing Robert Dakin. A man born to a violent life.

They approached the villa at last and turned into its encircling palm-bordered drive. She was preoccupied; she did not notice the lights were on in the house—more lights than were usually left at night. She got out of the car; Armand held the door for her and she hated the thought of his gaze upon her, knowing what he knew. The door of the house was flung open and a man came out and quickly down the steps toward them.

"Hello, Elizabeth. Hello, Uncle Bob."

It was Dyke.

She saw that. And in the same instant a woman, dark and slim, and chic in smart black traveling dress, came out the door too and stood, smiling, beside him.

"Here's Ruth," said Dyke. "She came with me."

5

THERE WAS a small flurry of greeting; yet the little scene was so sharp and clear that Elizabeth was aware, even, of the white gravel before the steps, the blue-black shadows of hibiscus and, as clearly and sharply, of a ladder, thin and starkly outlined in black, leaning against the wall of the house a little distance away from the steps. She must have given Dyke her hand; Robert had the woman in his arms and was kissing her heartily.

Dyke said, "It's Ruth Reddington. Ruth, this is Elizabeth."

The woman disengaged herself from Robert's arms. She had large, intelligent black eyes and smooth black hair and a translucently white skin, and she came forward and put out her hand toward Elizabeth.

Ruth? thought Elizabeth.

"You've heard of Ruth," said Robert Dakin impatiently. "Ruth Reddington. Practically my right arm."

"Yes, of course. I'm glad to see you. Won't you—perhaps we'd better go in."

Leech held the door for them; Dyke was talking rapidly. "Surprised, Uncle Bob? We had reservations on the boat. Then we found we could get the Clipper from Miami and come by car together from Kingston. We stayed in Kingston last night and came on to Montego Bay today."

Major Dakin in sudden, high—too high—good humor was leading the way into the drawing room, was ordering highballs for all of them, was pulling Ruth down on the divan beside him and patting her hands and smiling at her. "How long can you stay?"

Ruth made some reply. And Elizabeth slipped back her wrap and let herself look at Dyke.

He was exactly as she remembered him; gracefully easy in motion, his smile and his dark eyes quick and gay. His skin was brown, naturally brown but tanned, too; and she remembered with almost painful clearness the curve of his cheek when he smiled, the youthful look of his lips, the little frown that came in his forehead when he lifted his black eyebrows as he was doing then, the gaiety and charm in his smile and in his laughing eyes. There was, always, a kind of boyish impetuousness about him, which made him seem younger than in fact he was.

"We came mainly about the helium thing," he was saying.

And Ruth added, "We brought all the reports along. I wanted a trip so I came too."

37

"You wanted to see me," chuckled Robert—only a little too loudly, but Ruth's fine black eyes became a little fixed and Dyke's face was very still for a moment. "Confess it, Ruthie. You wanted to see me."

"Of course I wanted to see you. You've not been home—or even so near home as this since . . ." she stopped, and quickly, Elizabeth felt, substituted; she'd been about to say "since your marriage." She actually said, ". . . oh, it must be two years or so. You've gained in weight," she added quickly and crisply and accusingly. It pleased Robert Dakin. "Go ahead, scold me. Nobody else can keep me in line."

Ruth didn't smile. She said, "It's not my business to keep you in line, Bob. Tell him about the helium, Dyke."

But Robert would have none of it. Leech came in with highballs and they must drink. They must celebrate. They would leave business till the next day. He had a highball in his hand by that time. He put his other arm around Ruth and pulled her heartily close to him and held her there. "You can't imagine how I've missed you. Here's a toast to beautiful Ruth."

"Don't be such an idiot," said Ruth sharply, and leaned a little against his great shoulder. There was the smallest stain of pink in her cheeks. Dyke said, "Ruth—and Elizabeth," and lifted his glass toward Elizabeth and smiled directly, deeply into her eyes.

Unexpectedly, she thought of Cyril—so vividly it was as if he had stepped into the room.

38

But it was Dyke she had written to. He said in a low voice, speaking only to her, "You see, I came."

That was all, for Robert's hearty voice boomed through the drawing room so that even the crystal chandeliers seemed to vibrate.

"Prettier than ever, Ruth," he was shouting. "You ought to have a salary raise. How long has it been . . ."

Ruth cut in sharply. "Nonsense. You pay me too much already, Bob. When I went to work for you it was at ten dollars a week."

"Those were the days, eh, Ruth?"

"Twenty-five years ago, now, Bob."

"Twenty-five!" He was lounging heavily back against the sofa, still with one great arm hugging Ruth's slender, smart, black figure against him. Now he turned to look at her and frown. "Twenty-five! It isn't possible."

"It's true, nevertheless." Her dark eyes, almost velvety under long, jet black lashes regarded him steadily and inscrutably. Her skin was so white that her eyebrows looked like thin, jet black lines inked in by a delicate hand. Her features were aquiline and full of character and extremely regular; her mouth firm but well made up. She wore her shining black hair cut very short in the back with a high, smooth wave rising from her broad white forehead. She was beautiful, but there was no softness about her beauty —or in her poised and efficient manner. She looked, indeed, fully prepared to face life on any terms. She said now, looking at Robert, "Quite true, Bob. I was seventeen when I went to work for you."

"Yes." His face became sober, showing the sagging, flabby muscles as it didn't when he smiled. "Yes, I remember you, Ruth. Pretty as a picture. Lively, laughing. You had red cheeks in those days. And smart—more brains in your little finger than all the rest of my staff."

She smiled a little.

"There weren't so many in those days, Bob."

"No. You're right about that. We've come a long way, Ruthie. Let's drink to it." He lifted his glass and Dyke said, again in a low voice, so the others, talking again, could not hear, "I see what you mean. He's going to pieces."

Elizabeth thought of the two years just past: the doctors, the failures. The thing that had made those inevitable failures had been Robert's own will.

"But he could still pull out of it," added Dyke, "if he wanted to. By his looks I'd say he was about due for another . . ."

Again suddenly—inexplicably in the lighted room with others present—a familiar cold little wave of apprehension caught at her, and plucked at her nerves and quickened her breath. And Robert pulled himself heavily from the sofa.

"Ruth tells me you've got a batch of reports, Dyke. She thinks they'd better be put away."

"Right you are, Uncle Bob."

The two men walked together out of the room.

Elizabeth could hear their voices and the butler's and the shuffle of bags.

She looked at Ruth and Ruth was looking at her. Very quietly, very intently.

"So," said Ruth slowly, "you are Elizabeth."

6

It gave Elizabeth a rather disconcerting sense of repetition. Who else—why Charmian had spoken like that! Had looked at her like that.

"Dyke tried to describe you," said Ruth coolly. "But I didn't expect you to be so young. Why, you're a baby."

"I'm twenty-five."

Ruth's shining, slim eyebrows went up.

"I'm forty-two. You see, you are a baby. Bob's drinking a lot, isn't he? You don't need to tell me; I can see for myself. You must love him very much."

It took Elizabeth by surprise; so she found no quick and ready response to the words or to the long, deep—inquiring?—look Ruth gave her. Then Ruth continued smoothly, "Otherwise you wouldn't stick it out. I know Bob when he's drinking. Well," she turned the subject with almost a contemptuous directness, "I see you are wearing the emeralds."

Elizabeth's hand went to the jewels. Robert and

Dyke returned, and the talk became general for a few moments before they all went upstairs together.

"I'll ring for a maid to unpack you," said Elizabeth, but Ruth refused it, smiling, and looking about the room where her bags had been taken as if she remembered it.

There was a little confusion of good nights. Robert lingered, talking, in the doorway of Ruth's room and was still there when Elizabeth left them and went through his study as she had to do to reach her own suite.

Her rooms and Robert's were built in a long line comprising the entire northern wing of the second floor; the only entrance to it was the door from the main hall into Robert's study. And from his study—like a hall except that it was so wide—doors led to his own bedroom at the west, and thence to his own bathroom, and to the tiny passage that ran between Elizabeth's dressing room on the east, and her bathroom occupying the same space directly opposite, and thus to her wide, many-windowed bedroom, extending the width of the wing. This room opened at the north with wide French doors upon the balcony.

Passing through the study, now, and into the small passage of her own suite, she closed the door from the study behind her.

She undressed quickly and mechanically, taking off the emeralds and putting them in a little heap on the mirrored table in her dressing room.

In her big bedroom she opened the French doors

and stepped out on the balcony, pulling her heavy dressing gown tight around her. The night was dark with a few stars and so quiet she imagined she could hear the sound of the sea.

It was no good trying to think; there was no way to know what Robert Dakin was likely to do. But it was no good, either, clinging to the now frayed and battered ideals with which she had entered upon marriage. Because it had never been, really, a true marriage. She saw, then, for the first time that Robert had never belonged to her as he had belonged to Charmian—to Ruth.

She turned at last, chilled, and went into her bedroom and tried to sleep and could not.

It must have been very late when Robert opened the door of her bedroom. She sat up, her heart pounding.

"Elizabeth—I want the emeralds. Give 'em back to me."

"Why, I—certainly, Robert. They are on the table in my dressing room."

She pushed aside the folds of mosquito netting and turned on the light on the table beside her. He blinked and rubbed his eyes; his collar was open and his black tie hanging in strings; his thick hair was disheveled and his face was terribly lax and white.

"Hurry up. Go and get them. I want the emeralds."

She put her feet into slippers and took her dressing gown. She had to steel herself to pass him but he made no move to touch her, only followed her into the little dressing room.

The jewels lay on the table, winking back, reflecting a hundred lights in green. She put them into his hands.

"Are they all there?" He blinked and said, "I can't see. Are you sure you gave them all back to me?"

"Yes, yes. Really, Robert. All of them are there. The necklace—see . . ." She held it up for him to look at. "The bracelet—two rings."

He took her suddenly by the arm, leaning close to her, shaking her a little. His hand was heavy and strong; without meaning to, she pulled a little away from him and he gave a savage jerk which brought her back toward him. But his only thought was still the emeralds.

"If you're lying to me . . ."

"I'm not lying."

"I want to give them to somebody else." A slow grin twitched at the corners of his purplish mouth. "Somebody . . ." he repeated, half mumbling. And then he turned, wavering a little as a great tree, rotten at the core, wavers in the wind. She was often desperately sorry for him, and she was then. But she was also afraid. However, without another word, he walked back into his study and closed the door.

She waited a moment and heard no sound other than footsteps.

Back in her bedroom again she lay for a long time,

45

thinking but listening, too, for sounds along the passage. But he did not return.

Early the next morning, with the gay tropic sun pouring down on the balcony, as bright and golden as if the dark and quiet night had had no shadows, she saw Dyke for a few moments alone. She was on the balcony. Purple bougainvillea overhung the railing; away below the blue Caribbean sparkled and shone, and along the winding avenue leading from the gates to the house great Royal Palms flung themselves boldly against a cerulean sky. And Dyke came strolling along the lawn below, looked up and saw her.

"What are you doing up there?"

"Having chocolate."

"All alone?"

"Yes."

"I'm coming up. Shut your eyes and turn your back while I say abracadabra . . ."

Half laughing, she did it. There was a scramble, and she turned in time to see him swing his legs over the wide balcony railing and sit there, his eyes bright and laughing.

"I could do that rather better when I was in my teens," he said and took her hand, and kissed it. "You're beautiful, Elizabeth. I'd almost forgotten..."

He hadn't changed. Yet she felt, oddly, a little shy and strange. "I'll ring for chocolate for you." She went back to the small table.

"No, no, I've had mine." He paused, watching her, and then drew up one knee and clasped it with his

46

hands, and turned to look out over the sunny blue sea. "I—I wanted to talk to you," he said. "About your letter, you know." He hesitated. And then said directly, "Elizabeth, please understand. You see, I came. But—there's nothing I can do about it. Just now, I mean. Right away. Today. Please—please tell me you do understand."

7

THE SUN was as golden, the sky and sea as blue, yet
for a moment it was as if there were something false
and chill, a shadow somewhere. As if there was no
warmth even in the white woolen dressing gown she
wore—monkish with its hood and its long sleeves and
the heavy silken cord around her waist—or the sunlight on her sandaled feet.

"You mean," said Elizabeth at last, "that you have
changed? It's quite all right, you know. Don't mind
saying so. It's been two years . . ."

He got down from the balustrade and came quickly
to kneel beside her. "Darling, you're so sweet and
silly. I love you—understand? I'm only saying"—he
caught her hands and held them tight—"I'm only saying we've got to wait. And I haven't changed. Look
at me. Can't you see I haven't changed? Look at me,
Elizabeth." He kissed her hands, each finger, slowly,
laughing at her with his eyes, as he did so; and then
put both arms around her so his black head was
almost against her shoulder. "Don't you see, dear

48

Elizabeth? When you married Uncle Bob I had to stop thinking about you as I had before. I loved you and we were going to be married. I know it hadn't been announced and perhaps, in so many words, it hadn't been settled between us. But that was the truth, nevertheless, until that day we quarreled. You called me a fortune hunter. Remember, Elizabeth?"

The bickering of that faraway day struck her now as having been altogether childish. She said rather wearily, "That doesn't matter, Dyke."

"Of course, it doesn't matter. Now then, dear, listen. It's important. You must wait and trust me and . . ."

"Dyke, he knows."

"Uncle Bob? You told him . . ."

"He guessed. Last night. I didn't mean to tell him. I burned your letter. I . . ." Her voice wavered and he said:

"It's all right, Elizabeth. Was he very—well, never mind. You were brave to tell him." He stared at the distant blue sea for a thoughtful moment, and then said, "Well, trust me for a little while. Remember, I love you. And wait . . ."

He paused as someone walked across Elizabeth's bedroom and got to his feet just as Robert Dakin stopped uncertainly between the open French doors and put up his hands to shade his bloodshot eyes from the bright sunlight. But he was freshly shaven and dressed and said quite clearly, "Oh, there you are, Dyke! Ruth's waiting for us." He looked at Elizabeth

49

and then at Dyke. His eyes grew more accustomed to the glare of the sun and took in every detail of the little scene. The corners of his purplish lips twitched a little. "Oh, yes," he said, "I nearly forgot. There's something else I want to talk to you about, Dyke. Any time will do, though; there's no hurry about it."

Dyke said at once, "Certainly, Uncle Bob. Where's Ruth? Downstairs?"

"Yes, in the library. Well, well, come along. I suppose I've got to listen to the whole thing and then you'll do as you please, you and Ruth."

"We'll do as *you* please," said Dyke pleasantly. "See you later, Elizabeth." His eyes said again, Trust me. I love you.

They went away, through the French doors and her bedroom.

Elizabeth, left alone, sat for a long time in the sunlight, staring at the limitless horizon, and not seeing it.

Dyke was right to counsel patience. He hadn't reminded her of it, but the truth was that he owed everything he had or hoped to have (for almost certainly he was Robert's heir) to his uncle. She was doing him and Robert an injury when she came between them. Why hadn't she realized that before? Why had she so blindly stretched out her hand for help—any help?

She must tell Robert that Dyke was not to blame for that frantic letter she had written. That was only fair to both of them.

50

And somehow, anyhow, she must dissolve her marriage with Robert. After that her life would be her own again. A new start, she told herself.

Dyke had said he loved her; had asked her to wait. She wouldn't let herself be caught and entangled in a perplexity that had come, like an invisible cloud, out of that bright and sunny morning. The thing to do was to go straight ahead on the course which was the only honest and clear course she could follow.

She began to plan; this time definitely. She must choose her time with Robert, watching his moods.

It did not occur to Elizabeth that there are barriers and there are depths impossible to chart and plumb in advance; and that the courts of law are still operative only after the fact, not before.

The day, after that, went on quietly.

Elizabeth dressed and went about her usual tasks.

Small, but not unusual things happened. She gave household orders, checked menus, wrote a few letters. Some time during the morning a man came to repair the wireless. The aerial needed changing, he said, and there was some trouble about finding the ladder. She caught only an echo of it as she walked around the house and came upon Leech and the electrician. She did not really listen or, then, remember the ladder she had seen, rather curiously out of place as a matter of fact, the night before.

Cyril did not come and did not telephone but she had not expected him.

Robert and Ruth and Dyke (and, of course, Charlie

Hawes) spent the entire day in the library. They did not even emerge for lunch but had it served in the library amid the masses of papers and reports.

It was not until she came down to dinner that apprehension returned swiftly like a dark wind swooping upon her. For, as she went down the stairs, the library door opened and Ruth—already dressed for dinner, poised and lovely—came out of the library and closed the door quickly behind her. Ruth was very white. She said tautly, "Is he always like this? When he drinks, I mean. This is horrible, Elizabeth. Worse than I've ever seen him."

"But he . . . I thought today . . ."

"He's been drinking all afternoon—drinking and pretending to listen to us—and drinking. He's not heard anything we've said. We tried to get him to stop . . ."

The library door opened again and Robert Dakin stood on the threshold. Stood there swaying, eyes bloodshot and a little crazy, staring at the two women. He was so big and so powerful and so obviously lost to himself, that there was something terrible and tragic about him. He discovered Elizabeth, frozen on the stairway, clutching the railing, and he laughed uproariously and shouted, "There you are! Come down here! You're my wife. I want you here with me." The look in his eyes, the laugh, the shout, were fantastic, like those of delirium.

"Bob," said Ruth, putting her hands on his arm. He shook her off with a heavy, abrupt motion. "I want

52

you here, Elizabeth, and I want Dyke. No, Ruth, you stay out of this. *Dyke . . .*" It was a bellow.

Charlie Hawes' anxious face appeared momentarily behind Robert and vanished quickly. Leech came from the dining room, running, his face white and anxious. He went to Robert and tried to take him by the arm and support him but Robert pushed him away. And Dyke came from the library behind Robert.

"Here I am," he said. "You'd better go to bed, Uncle Bob. You'd better get some sleep."

Robert tried to whirl around to face Dyke, wavered, and as Leech and Dyke both sprang to support him, he waved them back and caught at the casing of the door. Again Charlie Hawes, face white as his stiff white shirtfront, hovered anxiously in the doorway and shrank back as Robert shouted: "No, by God, not before I finish. Where is she? She was here a moment ago. Where is she?"

Dyke said, "Who, Uncle Bob?"

"Charmian. No, I mean my wife. The girl—Elizabeth—I've got to see her. I've got to do something . . ."

"Mrs. Dakin is right here, sir," said the butler. "Won't you let me help you to the couch, sir? You're not well."

Without any warning at all, rather quietly indeed, Robert's great fist shot out and caught the old butler on the side of the head. It was a crushing blow, inexpressibly brutal. Leech's black knees sagged and he slumped forward on the floor, and lay there without moving. It was swift and silent as a moving picture. Then Dyke caught Robert by the arm and swung him around, Charlie Hawes vanished completely, and Elizabeth ran down the remaining steps and across the hall to kneel beside the butler.

And several things happened all at once. Ruth, she thought, came to stand by her and someone—herself—said in a high voice, "Ring—the bell's over there by the door. Have them bring brandy—get the doctor . . ." But Ruth had moved to go to Robert and she and Dyke were trying to hold him. And then Robert had shaken them both off and had reached Elizabeth and was pulling her to her feet. And she was standing before him and he brought his great hand heavily across her face.

It was a staggering blow—so heavy that she fell back away from him and the room and the objects and people in it were blurred, swimming in flaring lights against darkness. She brought up against a high-backed chair and clung to it.

When the swimming lights and blackness cleared, they were standing in silence—Robert and Ruth and Dyke—and Leech still lay on the floor. Ruth was staring at Robert fixedly. Dyke, a little at one side, watched him too—tensely, for Robert's next move. Charlie was nowhere to be seen.

Then she realized that with one of those bewildering flashes of sobriety and clarity of which Robert was erratically capable, he was fully aware not only of what he had done but of what he intended to do. He was standing straight now, and didn't waver. His eyes were still bloodshot and unnatural but had partially lost their hazy, mad look. He nudged Leech's body with the toe of his shoe and said, "Ring for somebody to take him away. He'll come around. *I said ring!*"

Charlie Hawes stuck his head cautiously around the library door and jerked it back again, and Dyke rang.

"Bob, you'd better go to bed." Ruth tried to take his arm and again he thrust her away. He said loudly and clearly, "She's been letting Dyke make love to her. They . . ."

"That's not true," said Dyke. "Uncle Bob, you don't realize . . ."

"All right. Answer a straight question. Do you want to marry her, Dyke? I'll cut you off, you know; everything you've got comes from me, you young fool, and you know it. Well, say—do you want Elizabeth or my money?"

"I'm going to call a doctor. You're drunk, Uncle Bob . . ."

Ruth glanced at Elizabeth and moved her head slightly toward the stairway as if to counsel her escape. But Robert saw it, too. He came across to Elizabeth and took her hand and would not let go; he drew her across the hall toward the stairway.

"Now then, Dyke," he said. "Once and for all, do you want to marry Elizabeth? Do you want her?"

Dyke started forward, then stopped abruptly.

Ruth cried sharply, "Bob, you're out of your head. You don't know what you're doing."

And it was then that Robert did the unexpected thing. He thrust Elizabeth's hand through his arm and started heavily up the stairs, drawing Elizabeth along with him. They reached the top of the stairs and turned toward Robert's study. There was not a sound from the two below in the hall. Robert led her through the study and then with a sudden thrust of his arms which sent her reeling against the wall, pushed her into the little passage.

He paused there and said in a way that was almost reasonable, "I'll be back. Later. I'm going to teach you things you need to know. Go ahead and scream. Nobody will hear or care." His purple mouth sagged a little, loosely, so it belied the reasonableness in his voice. Then he closed the door and she heard the key turn in the lock.

She stood for a moment quite still; she was shocked not so much by the ugliness of the thing or by his threat as by the look in Robert Dakin's bloodshot eyes. For something quite inhuman and crafty and obsessed had momentarily peered out at her.

8

IT WAS, however, something after ten before she slipped what money she could find in her various pocketbooks into her small dressing case and closed it. There was not much money, unfortunately. When Elizabeth Coolman Dakin shopped there were always liberal charge accounts and she never carried much cash with her. Unluckily, too, her jewel case and, which was more important since she intended to leave the island, her passport, were in the safe in Robert's study, and he was still there. She knew that, for she had gone at intervals to listen at the door and he was mumbling to himself as he often did when he was drinking.

She was going to leave; she had it planned. She would go quietly to the garage, take the small car and drive into town and to a hotel. The next day she would hire a car and driver and go to Kingston; from there by plane to Miami was only five or six hours. She would let lawyers settle the thing with Robert.

There was only the small, immediate problem of getting quietly out of the house; and if Dyke could ascend to the balcony by way of the bougainvillea, she could certainly get down the same way. She went out onto the balcony to make sure her way was clear.

It was very dark; but—across the bay—there were the lights of the town. And it was very still. She leaned further out from the balcony railing, trying to remember exactly how much of a drop it was to the ground. And something moved in the darkness below.

Because of the darkness perhaps, that movement, whatever it was, had a definite quality of stealth. It was not a footstep; it was not anything she could describe unless—she listened and was sure of it. Someone down there in the soft darkness was dragging something heavy across the grass. There was no other explanation for that special kind of soft, slithering sound. Something—what? And then she thought it must be Dyke come to rescue her—trying to help her; not defying Robert openly for fear of making things worse for her—and she leaned over the balcony rail and called softly, "Dyke—here I am—Dyke . . ."

The slithering sound stopped, but no one spoke. And there was all at once a strong sense of surveillance—of eyes somewhere in the soft darkness watching her. Instinctively, she drew further back into the heavy shadow of the bougainvillea and listened.

But moments passed and there was still no further sound from below. And she must hurry.

58

She shivered a little in the chill night; she must change her dinner dress to something less conspicuous. She had forgotten that. Soft gray taffeta swirled and whispered around her feet as she hurried again to her dressing room. This time, feeling as if Robert might surprise her before she could make her escape, she closed the door of the small dressing room; it had no key but she turned the flimsy bolt.

She would have to go without her passport. Besides, even if she could have gone to the safe she didn't know how to open it. The important thing was to leave.

She snatched a dark street dress and coat and hat from the cupboards that lined the room and then tried to unfasten her dress. But the hooks caught and entangled themselves; all at once she felt frantic, as one does in a nightmare confronted with insuperable odds and working against time.

Another hook evaded her. She was trying to find it amid the concealing taffeta folds when there was a great reverberating crash of sound which was almost immediately followed by another and louder repetition of the same sound. And they were both revolver shots.

Her fingers froze on the fastening of her gown.

Revolver shots? In Robert's study? What—who . . .

She was standing perfectly still and rigid. But she must move. She must inquire. She must do something. Revolver shots . . .

She turned swiftly and her hand struck a crystal

59

lamp on the table which went over with a loud crash. But not so loud as those shots had been. Not so terribly shocking.

She must pull herself together.

There is something paralyzing about the unexpected and unexplained sound of revolver shots. Elizabeth thought she was cool and thought she moved rather quickly. It was actually all of fifty or sixty seconds before she tried to open the door of her dressing room, forgot she had bolted it, fumbled with that little bolt and let herself out into the tiny passage.

She forgot, too, that Robert had locked the door into the study, for she turned instantly to that door and clutched the handle and it opened. So it was not, then, locked.

She couldn't explore the strangeness of that. For Robert was sitting at his desk—rather, he had fallen over upon his desk—with his head in his hands.

There was no one else in the room. The desk lamp spread a mellow, clear area of light upon the man sprawling there below it.

Her taffeta skirt rustled in that silent room—silent except that her ears still seemed to be full of the reverberating sounds of shots.

She must have gone to Robert for she was beside him, her hand upon his great shoulder. And there was blood—a great deal of blood.

She didn't scream. She cried, "Robert—Robert!"

There was a wound in his head and blood on his face. There was blood, too, on his white shirtfront and

60

his hands groped toward it. For he wasn't dead. His glazed eyes were half open and he mumbled, "Elizabeth—shot me—help . . ."

"Robert—Robert—I'll get the doctor . . . I'll get . . ."

"No, no. Don't—leave me. . . ."

The words came out slowly, dragging their way.

But she must get a doctor. Towels to staunch that blood. She turned toward his bedroom and bathroom, thinking of towels. And his great hand came out fumblingly but still strong and grasped her wrist.

"Stay—with me—don't go . . ."

"Robert, I must call the doctor. Let me go . . ."

People were running in the main hall, outside the opposite door from the study, which was closed. She was aware of their footsteps, of voices.

His hand gripped her wrist tighter. "Charmian—don't go—want to tell you—don't go—*listen* . . ."

There was such urgency in his slurred and dragging voice that she said, "Yes, yes, Robert. But you must let me go . . ."

His hand tightened. "Wait—got to tell you. You were wrong . . ."

His voice stopped in his throat with a kind of rattle, his eyelids wavered.

She tried to loosen his fingers on her wrist and failed. Someone was pounding at the door into the hall; why didn't they come and help her?

"I didn't do it," said Robert with a tremendous effort. His eyes flared open again and he looked directly at her. And said, "Charmian—no, I mean Elizabeth—good sport—sorry, my dear . . ."

And closed his eyes as if very weary.

His hand on her wrist relaxed its grip—slowly as she watched him. It fell heavily downward.

And Elizabeth screamed. She screamed and screamed again.

Someone beyond the closed door into the main hall was calling to her. Several people. They were telling her to open the door, to unlock it. She went to the door. The key was in the lock and she turned it and Ruth and Charlie Hawes stood there—staring, questioning, all at once silent as their eyes went past her. Then Ruth ran across the room and leaned over the sprawled body there at the desk.

Charlie Hawes cried, "Mrs. Dakin—oh, Mrs. Dakin —what happened—we heard the shots—who . . ."

And Dyke came, running, into the room, brushing Charlie aside as he too went to stand beside Ruth and look at the thing there across the desk.

Charlie, his rabbity face quite green and sick-looking, hovered beside Elizabeth.

Dyke cried, "Ruth—is he dead?"

"Bob—Bob . . ." said Ruth in a voice of anguish.

"Don't touch him. Let me—he's dead; there's no pulse. Good God, the blood everywhere! What happened? Who did it? Did he shoot himself? Where's the gun?"

There was a little silence. Charlie Hawes, beside

62

Elizabeth, stretched his thin neck to peer over Ruth's shoulder and went greener than ever.

Ruth said, "Gun? There's no gun here. Ask her. Ask Elizabeth. She found him."

Dyke said quickly, "Ruth—we'd better get a doctor."

"The police," said Ruth.

"But you—oh, for God's sake, Ruth, help me think." Dyke didn't move, just stood there staring down with his black shoulders outlined against the light from the desk lamp.

Charlie Hawes, apparently struck with the idea of finding the gun, began to creep timidly about the room, looking under cushions and chairs and avoiding the desk. And Ruth went around the desk and dropped down on her knees beside the supine bulk in the great chair and Elizabeth thought she was going to take him in her arms.

But Dyke said sharply, *"Ruth*—Ruth, he's dead! Don't you understand we've got to do something? Here—you'd better have a drink . . ."

Ruth just knelt there, huddled together like an old woman, staring. And Elizabeth knew there was something she had to do, so she moved toward them and her taffeta skirt rustled sharply in the stillness and she said, "I didn't kill him."

Only Charlie looked at her or apparently heard her and he only shook his head dismally. Dyke had gone to a table and was pouring something out of a bottle. He went to Ruth and put a glass in her hands and

63

said, "Drink that. Quick. We've got to pull ourselves together." He looked around then and saw Elizabeth and shoved a glass into her hand, too. It was cold against her fingers and when he said loudly, "Drink that. Drink it . . ." She did so.

Dyke was drinking, too—standing there again, watching the dead man as if hoping for orders. He was, as a matter of fact, thinking desperately, and Elizabeth realized that though she couldn't yet think herself.

Ruth put her glass down on the floor beside her and rose and put her hands upon the sodden thing there, half in the chair, half upon the desk. Then, as if shrinking from the blood, convinced at last of his death, her hands fell away and she dropped down on her knees again and in a queer gesture put her silky black head against his knee exactly as a dog might have done.

Elizabeth heard herself explaining, "I heard the sound of the shots. I came out and into the study and there he was."

Again only Charlie, pouring a quick drink for himself, paused politely to listen. Dyke said, "Suicide. How about it, Ruth? Suicide."

Ruth didn't lift her head; her eyes were closed and her mouth a shrunken red line. Dyke put down his glass and went around the desk and put his hand on Ruth's shoulder. "Ruth, get up. Ruth, you've got to help. *Ruth!*"

He pulled her to her feet. "Don't you understand,

Ruth? Suicide's the only answer. The servants will be here in a moment; we've got to call the police. Ruth, what shall I do?"

She did open her eyes then. She said, "Do? There's only one thing to do." And looked at Elizabeth. "She found him. She was alone with him. Ask her who shot him."

9

DYKE SAID, "It doesn't matter who did it, Ruth. It's done. Can't we make it look like suicide? Everybody knows what he was like when he was drinking . . ."

"Bob Dakin wouldn't commit suicide. Anybody who ever knew him would know that."

"But it's the only way, Ruth. Don't you see what a mess . . ."

She cast one long look about the room. "He was shot. We heard the shots. Where's the revolver that shot him?"

Charlie Hawes gulped and said it wasn't in the room.

"Unless," suggested Charlie, "it's—on the desk. Under him." His tone intimated that he didn't intend to look.

Dyke did so, reluctantly, shifting that heavy body. "It isn't here," he said finally.

Ruth turned swiftly to Elizabeth, "Where is it? What did you do with it?"

66

"But I didn't have it. You must listen to me. You must believe me. I didn't kill him. I didn't shoot him. I heard the sound . . ." Again, nightmarishly, it was exactly as if they didn't hear her. But Ruth did hear something in the hall, for she listened and went to the door and said uncertainly, "Dyke, who . . . ?"

And Cyril Kirby stopped in the doorway. He said, "I thought I heard—the door was open so I came right in . . ." and then he saw Robert.

"Cyril," cried Elizabeth unsteadily, and added, "Dyke—it's Cyril Kirby. Cyril, he's dead. He was shot . . ."

Cyril gave her one quick look and went to the desk and bent over. There was a little silence and then he straightened up, glanced at Ruth and at Dyke and said, "When did this happen?"

"Just now. We heard the shots. Then Elizabeth screamed."

He turned around then and came to Elizabeth. "You'd better sit down somewhere—here." There was a sofa near and he drew her toward it and sat down beside her and took her hands, "Now listen, Elizabeth. Tell me quietly just what happened."

"She shot him," said Ruth stiffly.

"Yes, I heard you saying that as I came up the stairs." He glanced at Dyke. "You must be Dyke," he said. "I've heard Major Dakin speak of you."

Dyke started forward, "We've got to do something. There was this shot and—it was suicide."

67

Cyril's sandy eyebrows lifted a little; he said, "Then we'll have to find the weapon."

"But it isn't in the room. And she won't tell . . ." It was Ruth.

Cyril glanced at her and said peremptorily: "Sit down." After a few seconds she did so, stiffly. Cyril said, "Was he drinking?"

He looked at Dyke, and Dyke, looking sick and gray, said, "Yes. Hard. I still think suicide . . ."

"You'd better sit down, too," said Cyril. "We've only a few minutes. The servants will be up . . ." He paused, and added quickly, "They ought to have heard the shots, too; unless they're in the other end of the house. Where's Leech?"

"He—was injured," said Dyke and swallowed. "Uncle Bob knocked him out. He's not come around yet—or hadn't a while ago when I inquired. He's been drinking all day—Uncle Bob, I mean . . ."

"I know. Now then, Elizabeth, can you talk? Exactly what happened?"

"I heard the shots. I was in my dressing room. I came out . . ."

"Right away?"

"I—I don't know. No, not right away. After a minute or so. I came into the passage and—into the study . . ."

"No one else was in the room when you came in?"

"No. Nobody."

"And he was dead?"

Elizabeth moistened her lips. "No." She was aware
68

that everyone looked at her quickly and with the sharpest attention when she said that. Even Charlie Hawes, fading into the shadow by the window curtains, jerked his rabbit face around to stare at her.

Dyke said tensely, "What do you mean? Did he talk? Did he say anything?"

Cyril laid his hand over her own. "Steady, Elizabeth. Go on."

"He wasn't dead. His eyes were open. I told him I would get a doctor. He held my wrist—he wouldn't let me go. I thought I'd get towels to stop the bleeding."

"But what did he say?" demanded Dyke. "Didn't he talk? Didn't he tell you . . . ?"

"Did he talk, Elizabeth?" asked Cyril gently.

"Yes. But he—he didn't say much. He was rambling and—and incoherent. Except at the last he—he called me by my right name and I think tried to say he was sorry. About us, he meant. And then he died."

"But, Elizabeth," cried Dyke, "didn't he tell you what happened? Didn't he tell you who shot him? Didn't you ask him?"

"No. No, I never thought of it. He—" she turned to Cyril. "He didn't tell me who shot him. All I thought was that I must get help—do something for him. And he held my wrist—oh, please believe me."

"Quite," said Cyril definitely. "We do believe you, Elizabeth."

There was a little silence. Dyke got up, walked across the room, lighted a cigarette with a sharp sputtering of a match and went back to stand behind the chair in which Ruth sat; he leaned on its high back and stared at the carpet. And Cyril said in a quiet and rather gentle voice, "Don't be frightened, Elizabeth. Try to think. Is that all that happened?"

"Yes. Yes, Cyril."

"You heard only the shots—no voices, no footsteps?"

"Not then. A little while before that I heard Robert mumbling to himself. I'm sure it was Robert."

"Did you hear words? What did he say?"

"Nothing that I could distinguish. I had just packed . . ."

Ruth got up out of her chair. "Packed?" she said.

"Yes. Yes, I was going away. I had put things in my bag and I was just going to change my dress when I heard the shots."

Her dress was falling off her shoulders; Cyril said absently, "Turn around." She turned so he could reach the little hooks and he fastened it carefully, talking, "Take your time, Elizabeth; think about it. You must have heard someone here in the study."

"Mr. Kirby, I don't know who you are or what you're doing here. But I do know you're trying to put words into her mouth. If she shot him . . ."

It was Ruth again and the steel in Cyril's eyes got suddenly into his voice. He said, "Exactly. *If* she shot him. Might I ask who you are and what you're doing here?"

Dyke murmured in a conventional way that seemed

fantastically out of place just then, "Miss Redding-ton—Ruth, this is Mr. Cyril Kirby . . ."

Ruth herself said at the same time, "I am Ruth Reddington. I have—worked for Bob for twenty-five years. I have a right to be here and to ask questions. And I'll decide what we are to do."

Dyke murmured again, "That's right. Ruth always knows what's best, Kirby. We'd better let her take charge . . ."

Cyril fastened the last hook and said briefly, "We'll do exactly as Elizabeth says to do."

Dyke glanced uneasily toward the desk, went into Robert's bedroom and returned with a sheet which he began to arrange over the body. They all watched, irresistibly, as he did it and thus saw the little start he gave as he bent again over the body. For it was just then that he found the very curious thing he did find.

"What is it?" said Cyril sharply as Dyke took some small object in his fingers.

Dyke did not reply and Cyril went to him and Ruth turned to look, too.

"It's nothing," said Dyke, then, quickly, "just a—a keepsake, I imagine."

"Elizabeth, did you ever see this before?" asked Cyril. And held the small object so she could see it.

It was a very small wooden image of the three warn-ing monkeys—one with its little paws over its ears, one with its paws over its eyes, one with its paws over its mouth. She remembered having seen such groups, here and there commonly, in her childhood. She remembered the adage they were supposed to represent. Hear no evil, see no evil, speak no evil. But she had never seen that particular small wooden image before. Certainly she had never seen it in Robert's possession. She said so at once. "How about you, Miss Reddington?" asked Cyril.

Ruth was looking at it, frowning. "I can't remember," she said slowly. "I've seen those monkeys—many times. They used to be very popular, you know, as parlor bric-a-brac. It's been years since I've seen one." She paused, still frowning, and then looked with what seemed frankness at Cyril. "It does seem vaguely familiar to me," she said. "But I can't possibly say why. Unless, of course, it belonged to—him—and was, as Dyke said, a keepsake."

"Was it here on the desk when you found him, Elizabeth?" asked Cyril.

"I don't know. I didn't see it. But I—wouldn't have noticed."

"I see," said Cyril. "Well—we'd better put it back on the desk for the police."

"Police," said Charlie Hawes with a gasp.

"Why, certainly," said Cyril. "The sooner the better. We've wasted too much time already. Every minute gives—whoever shot him—that much more chance of escape." He took up the telephone.

And Ruth drew herself up into a semblance of her usual poise and said coolly, "I think you'd better know, Mr. Kirby, that the door from this room into the hall was locked on the inside. We had to wait out-

72

side, after we heard the sound of the shots, until Elizabeth chose to unlock the door. And since she claims that she was in her own suite immediately beyond this room, and saw no one, and it is a twenty-five foot drop from the windows to the terrace, exactly how do you think the murderer escaped?"

Cyril did not reply, for he was saying quickly into the telephone, "I want the police. I don't know the number. Give me the Inspector. Hurry. It is murder."

10

"Theey'll come at once." Cyril put down the telephone and turned to Ruth. "Miss Reddington."

She looked at him but did not reply or move. He went to her and said quietly, "I remember now. I'm sure I've heard the Major speak of you."

Again she did not reply, only watched him.

Cyril said directly, "About this locked door."

This time Ruth said, "Yes, I thought you were coming to that. You want us to say nothing about the locked door, is that it? We are to protect Elizabeth—is that to be our program?"

"We'd better have no misunderstanding, Miss Reddington. Do you believe Elizabeth shot Major Dakin?" asked Cyril.

"It isn't a question of what I believe. There was no one else here. She has just said she intended to leave him, that she was packing . . ."

"Yes," said Cyril. "That's another thing." He looked at Elizabeth. "Go in your dressing room and unpack your bag. Put everything away in its usual place, but do it quickly. As quickly as you can."

She saw the reason for that. But first she must make them understand. "You must believe me," she said almost frantically. "I didn't kill him. I heard the shots and I . . ."

Dyke looked at the carpet. Ruth interrupted her, "Besides, there's the gun, Mr.—er—Kirby. Where is it?"

"But I . . ." began Elizabeth. Cyril said, "Go on, Elizabeth. Hurry. There's no time . . ."

He was right, of course.

"Miss Reddington—Dyke," began Cyril as she went, "if you really believe Elizabeth shot him, then of course there's nothing for you to do but tell the police about the locked door and that you believe she killed him. But if there's any doubt in your minds you must give yourselves and Elizabeth a fair chance. Do you really believe that girl shot him?"

By that time Elizabeth had reached the little dressing room, but she could hear their voices even as she bent, automatically removing dressing gown, removing clothing and toilet things which she had flung in that case only a short time ago.

There was a silence in the next room. Apparently no one intended to answer Cyril's question. Finally, Charlie Hawes said, "The servants . . ."

"They won't know about that."

"They know he was drinking." That was Dyke's voice.

Cyril said, "You agree with me, though."

There was another pause. Elizabeth found herself folding stockings painstakingly and told herself she must hurry, and thrust them in the drawer.

Then Dyke's voice said slowly, "He's perfectly right, Ruth. It's going to be bad enough, any way you look at it. The newspapers—you never know where a thing like this will end. No use in telling any more than we have to tell."

"If she didn't kill him, who did?" It was Ruth's voice.

"If we could tell them it was suicide . . ." began Dyke.

"But the gun isn't here," said Charlie Hawes. "I've looked . . ."

"Suicide's out," said Cyril. "Open those windows, will you, Dyke."

Elizabeth hurriedly arranged a dress on a hanger. "Open the windows." That meant to make it look as if someone could have entered from the window, but that was absurd because there was a drop of at least twenty-five feet from window to lawn. They were moving about in the next room. Dyke said, "Ruth, I'm sure he's right. We'll tell only what we have to tell. Right?"

"You mean there's no need to tell them of your own trouble with Bob. Is that what you mean, Dyke?"

"I'm thinking of Elizabeth," said Dyke. "It would involve her."

76

Cyril said from the doorway near her, "Hurry, Elizabeth. Is the bag empty? Where does it go?"

She pointed to the shelf, and he closed the bag, fastened the cover quickly and lifted it to the shelf. He glanced swiftly around the dressing room, went to the chaise longue and pulled the folded coverlet at the foot of it awry, dented the pillows, took a magazine from the small table beside it, opened it and dropped it face down upon the floor. The lamp lay where it had fallen and he left it there. He took a cigarette from the box, lighted it and put it down in the ashtray. He glanced around the luxurious little room again and then came to Elizabeth. He put his hand under her chin and lifted her face.

"Look at me, Elizabeth, and pay attention to what I say. You've got to lie a little. Not much; there's no use in trying anything elaborate; we'd be caught up at a hundred points. But you've got to forget that locked door; understand? And, Elizabeth—if you have a gun of any kind, you'd better give it to me."

"I didn't . . ."

"Do you have a gun?"

"No. No, I've never had one."

"Good. Now then, remember; the door was not locked when Ruth and Dyke and Charlie came into the room. Understand?"

"Yes."

"And there was no trouble and you had not decided to go away and you had not packed your bag.

You were sitting here reading when you heard the shots."

"Yes—yes, I understand."

He searched her eyes and said after a moment, "I wish I could be sure of that. Elizabeth—you must pull yourself together. Think, before you answer the police. Don't let them trap you."

"I understand."

"I hope you do." He paused to listen. An automobile had apparently turned into the grounds and was approaching the house. It was followed by another. There were muffled sounds of car doors being slammed. Engines were cut off.

"Here they are," he said. "All right. Remember, Elizabeth. Keep your head."

Strange feet were entering the house; there were voices and commotion below.

He took her hand in a tight hard clasp and led her into the study again, just as three men appeared at the opposite door.

One was evidently a doctor, for he carried a doctor's bag and went at once to the body. Another, a sub-inspector, quickly and quietly began to search the entire double suite of rooms and the third, in plain clothes, began at once to inquire so tersely and pointedly about the general circumstances of the murder that it was impossible for them to give any but the briefest and clearest of replies.

Instinctively, Elizabeth felt that her fate, quite literally and truly, rested in a large measure with this man, and she was right, for he was Inspector Paul Friker, once of the London C.I.D. Because of a recurrence of an old lung weakness which had followed war gas, he had sought for and recently, when the post fell vacant, secured an inspectorship on the island, where the hot suns of the tropics were a welcome change from London winters. Besides basic intelligence and training, he had, added, a certain brilliance and hardness of his own like the polish and cutting of a diamond.

Physically he was slender and rather tall with narrow, fine bones. He had a small, vivid face, almost delicate in the fineness—and yet the hard clearness— of its features; there was a clear, red color high in his cheeks and in his lips; he was dark, with a small mustache and hard, brilliant black eyes. He had small hands, too, and dressed and carried himself with a certain inborn elegance which was not at all unsuitable or out of place. He belonged to a good and old family, he liked his work and always had, and he had to have the money it brought him. He was sensible and he was also intuitive; his strength lay in a certain trained and deliberate imperviousness to any appeal on the part of the suspects he dealt with, which might go further than impersonal sympathy and thus affect his thought or action regarding them. It was his business to extract a clear pattern of their lives and emotions, but to treat that pattern exactly as a scientist treats a slide under his microscope. He was by no means coldly inhuman; he only knew what he was after and was impatient of being swerved from that goal.

"Who was the murdered man?" he began. Robert Dakin. English? Oh, American. Who had murdered him? They didn't know. Was there anyone in the house besides themselves, and, of course, the servants? No one that they knew of. Had there been a thief? Was anything stolen? Then exactly what had happened? Who had found him? Oh, Mrs. Dakin. His eyes singled out Elizabeth without being told that she was Mrs. Dakin. Would she tell him, please, but quickly, the circumstances? When had she found him?

"A few moments ago—perhaps half an hour—I'm not sure—I was in my dressing room—I heard the shots . . ."

"How many?"

"Two. I came out and he was lying across the desk."

"Was anyone in the room?"

"No. I . . ."

"What did you do?"

"I went to him. I tried to . . ."

"He was dead then?"

"No."

"How long after did he die?"

"A—a minute or two. I'm not sure."

"Did he say anything to you?"

"Yes—but nothing that was coherent. He didn't tell me what had happened. He . . ."

"Then he died. What did you do?"

"I let . . ." She caught herself quickly. "That is, the others came in."

"Where is the revolver?"

He still addressed her, but Charlie Hawes peered around Dyke's shoulder and said, "It isn't in the room. I looked everywhere."

"That's why, you see," said Cyril, "we thought it was murder and not suicide."

Inspector Friker glanced quickly around the room, went to the desk, said something in a low tone to the doctor and then turned toward them again. "Will you kindly wait a few moments," he said, "in another room?" And nodded briefly to the sub-inspector who entered just then from Robert's bedroom.

Elizabeth had been consciously avoiding a glance toward the desk where the doctor bent over Robert. She turned with the others toward the door. But the sub-inspector apparently understood something unspoken in Mr. Friker's direction. For she was politely but quickly separated from the others so that she did not actually realize it until the door of the library closed and she found herself alone, except for a uniformed policeman who had turned up from somewhere in the lower part of the house—for the house and grounds had been quietly searched while Friker questioned them. There had not been time, even, for another word with Cyril. But then, with policemen around them, what could she have said?

After a moment, realizing she could do nothing but wait, realizing, too, that the uniformed policeman standing at ease near the door intended to stay there, she went to a chair and sank into it.

Sank into it, indeed, as flabbily as a doll with the stuffing taken out of it.

It was very quiet in the spacious, cool library with its polished floor and light rugs and high ceiling; she could hear little of what went on in the rest of the house. There were footsteps now and then in the hall; an occasional murmur of voices but that was all.

And it was no good thinking. After a while, lifting her face from her despairing hands, she told herself that. There was, even, no protecting sense of un-reality. Robert was dead—shot—murdered. She discovered a smear of red, now turning faintly brown, on the front of her dress to prove it.

Probably they had seen that. She seemed to remember a quick, direct glance of the inspector's brilliant black eyes.

What came next? Would they question the others first? What would Ruth say? What would Dyke say? What damaging facts of her life with Robert Dakin would they extract from timorous, uneasy Charlie Hawes?

She began to perceive a hundred avenues leading to danger.

I I

SHE ROSE and paced the floor and began to plan; trying to cover contingencies—if they asked this she
must answer thus.

She fixed definitely, deliberately, in her mind the
things Cyril had warned her about; she must remember that she was reading when she heard the shots—the
door from the study into the main hall was not
locked.

The police would eventually know something of
the ugly scene in the hall that night—and of other
equally violent scenes with Robert—the servants
would tell them; and there was Leech. Perhaps the
servants didn't know that Dyke had been a part of it.
But there was Armand, the chauffeur; he had heard
Robert's accusations on the way home from the hotel.
He had heard her tell Robert she intended to leave
him and had heard Robert oppose it—violently and
with threats. Robert's own voice echoed in her ears
suddenly, "I'll strangle you with my own hands . . ."

Would the chauffeur tell? In the hands of the police what a motive that would be!

Two pink spots began to burn feverishly in her cheeks. Her skirts rustled as her steps quickened and the policeman eyed her watchfully.

Then the police must not know about Dyke.

And it occurred to her, then, with an enormous sense of shock that perhaps Dyke had killed him. Robert had been in a state of violence to breed murder. And if Dyke had done it, it had been, actually, because of her.

She thought back, remembering the things Dyke had said and failed to say.

If he had done it, how had he escaped? The door from the study into the main hall had been locked on the inside—and there was no time, after those shots, for any manipulation of the key from the outside of the door. The windows were impossible as an exit. The only other possible exit was by way of the door into her own suite, and thence to the balcony and a descent by the vines as she had intended to go, and he had not gone that way, for she would have seen him.

Besides they were all—Dyke and Ruth and Charlie —pounding at that locked door, calling to her while Robert held her wrist and murmured incoherently. Time, again, would seem to prove Dyke's innocence. And it proved Ruth's, then, and Charlie's. She shook her head impatiently.

In any case, the police must not know about Dyke.

84

That was first; there was no time, then, to think of what might come later.

Still pacing nervously up and down, with her silk skirts whispering, and her small head high, she conned over the things she must say, the things she must not say. Once she caught a glimpse of herself in a mirror hung between long jalousied windows and scarcely knew the face that looked back at her. The small white face, with too bright eyes and too tight a mouth; she looked proud with her red hair high on her head and her slender white throat and shoulders rising almost regally from the low silk bodice—and she was as a matter of fact stiff with terror.

Time passed; the clock struck two before they came to question her.

The house had grown cool while she waited; she was not aware of it, but when Mr. Friker came into the library at last, followed by another uniformed policeman, he gave her one bright, hard glance and murmured some direction to the policeman, who went away and in a few moments returned with one of her own sweaters.

The inspector waited (deliberately taking out cigarettes, offering her one, without speaking, which she refused, and lighting his own) until the policeman returned. Then Mr. Friker took the sweater and came to her.

"May I . . ." he said and held it for her.

She had not realized how chilled she was until she

felt the soft wool jacket around her bare shoulders and arms.

"Thank you."

"Won't you sit down?"

She hesitated and then did so, clasping the arms of the chair tightly and looking up at the inspector. Funny that one's heart did, almost literally, get in one's throat!

The policemen disappeared, closing the door after them; the inspector went to the great, carved table in the middle of the room and sat on the corner of it, swinging one leg, smoking and looking at her.

"Madam," he said directly, "it will save time and effort for both of us if I inform you of certain things. Will you be so good as to listen?"

"I am listening."

"And please remember that anything I tell you I have the means of proving. I'll make no statement as a trap or as a trick." He glanced along the table, pulled an ashtray toward him and neatly deposited in it the ashes from his cigarette. "Now then. First. Your husband, Major Dakin, was a dipsomaniac; he was a victim of periodic drinking bouts during the course of which—and until he was ill enough to submit to the care of a doctor—he was extremely quarrelsome and violent. He began drinking hard yesterday and by dinner time tonight was fully launched upon an attack; so much so that just at dinner time there was a violent scene in the hall just outside this room, ending with his striking the butler and yourself. The

86

butler is still unconscious and the doctor, who looked at him, believes he has a slight concussion. After striking you, your husband took you forcibly to your own room and locked you there. What did he say to you then?" He slid the question so deftly and quietly into his speech that Elizabeth almost answered—irresistibly as one does a fortune teller.

She caught herself in time. "He was not himself. He was almost incoherent."

"What did he say?"

"He said—that he would return later. Something like that."

"What threats exactly did he make?"

Elizabeth replied carefully.

"He mumbled something about teaching me what I needed to know. He was not sensible of what he was saying and I knew it."

"Madam, will you please tell me the truth?"

"I am telling you the truth."

His hard, brilliant eyes revealed nothing. He continued, "You are thought to have remained in your room for some time. You were not seen again until the sound of the shots was heard and when the others came to the study they found you there with your murdered husband. Is that true?"

Elizabeth moistened her lips. "Yes, that is true."

"For your information I want you to know the position of the rest of the household. The servants—with the exception of the unconscious butler, Leech—were together in the servant's hall listening to the wireless; they knew nothing of the murder until the police cars arrived and each substantiates the others' alibis. Miss Reddington says she was in her own room writing letters; she heard the sound of the shots and came immediately to the study. Mr. Dyke Sanderson says he had just returned from a walk along the driveway and had entered the house and met Charlie Hawes; at his suggestion—Mr. Sanderson's, that is—both men had gone to the buffet in the dining room and were having a highball before going to bed. They were together when they heard the shots."

Then it couldn't have been Dyke. She heard it with such a poignant relief that she was afraid it would communicate itself telepathically to the man watching her. She tried not to show relief in her face and the inspector went on, "I'd better tell you, too, that the others of the household have been waiting in separate rooms and have not been permitted to speak to each other until after they were questioned. Mr. Hawes' and Mr. Sanderson's stories corroborated each other perfectly. Madam, are you paying attention?"

She was thinking, rather dreadfully, that left only herself and Ruth without an alibi. She said, "But I was locked in my room, Inspector. I . . ."

He didn't smile but the glitter in his eyes and vivid face might have passed for a smile—quick and a little scornful. "Oh, come, Madam! If the door from the study to your own suite was locked, how did you enter the study?" He put out his cigarette, got down from the table and came to a chair near her where he sat leaning back, putting his fine, sensitive-looking fingers together. He looked at her over the little tent his hands made and said, "Where is the revolver?"

"But I—I tell you I don't know. You must understand. I didn't murder him. I had no gun. I only heard the sound of the shots . . ."

"What were you doing when you heard the shots?"

"I was—was in my dressing room. I was reading. It is true that the door from my suite was unlocked when I opened it after I heard the shots. I don't know how that happened. I don't know who unlocked it. I suppose he—Robert—did it and I did not hear . . ."

"You mean he unlocked the door and there were further—words? Madam, if you were obliged to protect yourself—"

"Oh, no, no! You must believe me—he didn't—I don't know who unlocked the door or when. I only know that when I heard the shots and ran to the door it was unlocked and I went on into the study. I didn't —I couldn't stop then to question it."

She wished his small, fine face would change in expression. He said, "Madam, are you aware that under the circumstances I have mentioned there would be a question of justifiable self-defense?"

And he had said, thought Elizabeth bitterly, that he intended no trap. "But that did not happen," she said steadily. "I didn't kill him. And I don't know who did it."

"What were you reading when you say you heard the sound of the shots?"

"I—I don't know," she said rather desperately. "I was not paying much attention to what I was reading. Naturally, after what had happened . . ."

"You were thinking of your quarrel with your husband, you mean? You were not thinking of leaving the house? Leaving your husband, perhaps? Intending to divorce him?"

"I—I've told you exactly . . ."

"I beg your pardon, Madam, you have not told me exactly what happened. As a matter of fact, you spent some of the time between the quarrel with your husband and his murder in packing clothes in a dressing case. Now why did you do that?"

He paused, watching her, and she couldn't for a moment reply. How did he know? Did he really know, or was it a chance surmise?

He said, "Don't lie. I asked you not to lie, in the beginning. And I told you I could substantiate every statement I made." The expression in his face did change by the smallest degree then but showed only faint impatience. "When a perfectly neat wardrobe shows several street frocks all awry on their hangers, thrust anyhow into it; when jars of cosmetics are sadly out of place on an otherwise precise and well-arranged dressing table; when two or three pairs of stockings, bits of lingerie, a dressing gown, all show signs of having been hastily and untidily put away in an otherwise extremely neat and tidy dressing room,

90

I say to myself, why? These are the things a woman would take away with her if she went away quickly and wanted to take only a small bag which she could carry herself. How did you propose to escape, Madam? Since the door from your suite to the study was locked, and your husband sat there in the study and would almost certainly have stopped you?"

Again, staring back into his bright, hard eyes, she said nothing.

He went on with, now, a kind of disdain. "Someone helped you unpack your bag. Someone who lighted a cigarette and placed it carefully on the little table. Was that to look as if you had been quietly smoking—oh, yes, and reading; I must not forget that—when the shots were fired? Whoever did that does not use lipstick—as you do, Madam." He bowed a little so it was like a compliment. "Now then, Madam, will you kindly tell me who it was that unlocked the door from your suite to the study? Who it was that escaped through your rooms and down the trellis of vines—a good solid trellis and thick vines from the balcony to the ground? Who it is that you are shielding?"

"No one," cried Elizabeth sharply. "No one."

"Someone who must have known you were there and would help him escape. For you see, Madam, if the murderer had not known you would help, that murderer would not have entered your suite, knowing that you were there. Now then, who was it?"

"I tell you no one." She was leaning forward in her chair. "No one was there. I was alone . . ."

Again, almost, he smiled. "Alone. Very well. And Madam—how long was it after your husband died that you went to the other door—the door from the study into the main hall, unlocked that door and let others of the household enter the room? What did you do before you unlocked that door? Where did you hide the revolver?"

12

SHE COULD ONLY DENY.

"I had no revolver," said Elizabeth with stiff lips. "I did not kill him."

He seemed to sigh a little and unclasped his hands.

"Madam, let me beg you to consider your position. It is known that your marriage was an unhappy one; your servants were not disloyal to you in informing me; the truth came out in a dozen different ways. Besides, a young and—excuse me, Madam—beautiful wife married to a man many years her senior, and who is given to repeated, prolonged attacks of drinking during which he is both abusive and violent—all this carries its own significance. Where were you going?" Again the question slid quietly toward her with the persuasive, casual manner of a fortune teller, eliciting information so deftly, so adroitly that the victim is scarcely aware of it.

Elizabeth took refuge again in flat denial. "I didn't kill him. I don't know who killed him. I am shielding no one. It's as I have told you; I heard the shots, I went into the study . . ."

"Did he attempt to stop you when he learned you were going away? Did he oppose it?"

"He didn't know it." She stopped. She was appalled by the ease with which the admission had been drawn from her. It was like a bottomless pit opening at her feet. She had been confident of her own strength. She continued quickly, "I didn't see him or talk to him after I entered my own rooms until I heard the shots . . ."

"Madam, believe me, it is better for you to tell me the whole truth at once, without these attempts to evade. As I say, there is always the question of self-defense. How long have you known Cyril Kirby?"

The neat swerving of his line of inquiry, like the unexpected attack of a skilled fencer, caught her unprepared. "I don't know exactly. Perhaps a year or two."

"You met him after your marriage, then? Or you knew him before?"

"After."

"And Mr. Sanderson—your husband's nephew. Naturally you have known him for some time?"

"Yes."

"How long?"

"I—two or three years, I suppose."

"Since before your marriage, then?"

He could easily prove the truth. "Yes," said Elizabeth, feeling as if ice had settled around her heart.

He'd gone, then, from the damaging enough basis of opportunity and circumstance to the more damaging basis of motive. She thought of Dyke's letter to her with a swift thankfulness for having destroyed it. If they searched the house minutely as they would do—were even then perhaps doing—there was no shred of evidence that they could use against her.

But had they questioned the chauffeur? Had he told them the thing he knew? She waited, scarcely breathing, for the next question.

"You were very good friends, were you not?"

"Good friends, yes," said Elizabeth, keeping her voice level.

"Yet after your marriage, even with the close relationship that existed between Dyke Sanderson and your husband, you and Mr. Sanderson did not meet again until now. Why?"

"Because he was in America; we have only recently come here from England; he is in charge . . ."

"Yes, yes, I know all that," interrupted Inspector Friker. "Madam, what was the cause for the quarrel between yourself and your husband tonight?"

"C-cause?" said Elizabeth.

"Yes, certainly. Why did you quarrel?"

"Inspector Friker, a cause for a quarrel," said Elizabeth with rather sad truth, "was not always necessary with my husband."

"But there was a cause tonight. What was it?"

"The cause," said Elizabeth steadily, "was what it always was. Robert had been drinking; he was very

95

nervous and very irritable and he was not, really, aware of what he was doing. I should think his treatment of Leech, which was altogether unprovoked, would prove that to you." She essayed a small defensive of her own. "And it seems to me that it is a mistake to spend so much time questioning me. I don't know who killed him. You might better employ the time and energy searching for—for whoever it was that shot him and escaped."

"I assure you, Madam, that that is being attended to. You admit then that you had packed a bag, intending to leave the house, and that you then unpacked it—after your husband's death?"

"Inspector, I have tried to reply to your questions, fully and promptly whenever I thought my answers would help you find my husband's murderer. But I"—Elizabeth swallowed hard and went on as firmly as she could speak—"but I see that your questions are put mainly with a view to—to inducing me to admit things damaging to me. So I think I ought to have the advice of my lawyer." (What was the law? Could she refuse to talk?)

Mr. Friker smiled for the first time—a smile that was exactly as tight and hard as his look.

"Madam, will you come with me, please," he said, rising. "I want you to show me just where you stood when you heard the shot, just what you did—don't hesitate, Madam. Your husband's body has been removed."

That was, then, to re-enact what she knew of the

crime! Strangely, it seemed quite matter of fact and horribly real; not at all unreal and of a world one only read about in the newspapers, as it would have seemed, say, yesterday. She rose with a whisper of silk and went with him.

No one was in the hall although a servant—Flemming, the houseman—peered at her from the dining-room door.

The stairway, the corridor of the bedroom floor were also deserted. The sub-inspector was in the study and had evidently been taking records of finger-prints and measurements. At a nod from Friker he remained, moving quietly here and there about the room and in and out of the other rooms in the suite.

"Now, then, Madam, if you will be so good," said Friker. "Begin with your husband's locking you in your own suite. What, then, did you do?"

So she began. She had sat for a time in her bed-room. Doing nothing; thinking. After a long time she had—had gone to her dressing room.

"To pack your bag," said Friker. "You admitted that, you know."

"But I . . ."

"Madam," he said with again the sharp suggestion of impatience, "I warned you in the beginning that I made no statement I could not substantiate. When I questioned Miss Reddington she admitted that you had packed your bag intending to leave and had then, before I arrived, unpacked it."

"Ruth . . ."

He put up one small hand quickly.

"She did not volunteer the information. I had already come to the conclusion that this must have occurred. She only admitted it when I—let us go on, Madam. What was your husband doing during this time?"

Had Ruth been willing enough to tell it? Had he discovered also that the study was locked away from the rest of the house?

"Where was your husband during this time?" he repeated.

"He—he was, I think, in his study the whole time. I think so because once or twice I—listened at the door and I heard him moving about and talking."

"Talking?" said Friker sharply.

"Talking, I think, to himself. He did that sometimes when he was drunk."

"Did you hear any words?"

"No—nothing distinguishable."

"But you hadn't any doubt it was your husband?"

She hesitated, longing to say yes; failing to recall any faint impression of any other presence. He said sharply, "I see you had no doubt it was your husband until now. Go on, please. Where were you when you heard the shots?"

"I was—here . . ." She moved so as to stand in the middle of the little dressing room. "I was—I was intending to put on another dress. I was about to remove this one. I heard the shots and stopped—perfectly still for some time; I don't know how long; I was very much surprised—so surprised that I couldn't do anything for a few seconds. Then I realized what it must be—I turned and my hand struck the lamp on the table and it fell over on the floor. You see—" she pointed to the crystal-based lamp which lay at her feet.

He looked at the lamp without expression.

"And then . . ."

"Then I—I went into the study . . ."

"Show me."

She did so.

"You see, this door was then unlocked. I've told you that I don't know who unlocked it or when. But I opened it and—and he was there at the desk."

"And you did what?"

"I—went to him."

The chair beside the desk was empty now. There were stains, already dried, upon the top of the desk. She tried not to see the stains and not to see, mentally, the bulky thing that had lain there, but it was as if that image superimposed itself upon the now empty desk and chair.

The inspector lighted another cigarette.

"And he was not dead?"

"No. He died—after a minute or two." She was trembling a little and trying not to show it.

"Madam, believe me, I will try to be mercifully brief. He was conscious then; he spoke to you; what did he say?"

She tried to remember—broken phrases—rambling

—incoherent. She told him, word for word, as nearly as she could remember it.

Immediately he picked up the new name.

"Charmian?"

"His first wife. He often confused our names, particularly when he was drinking."

"You say your only thought was to get help?"

"Yes, yes—but he held my wrist; he wanted to talk. But he didn't tell me what happened; he didn't tell me who shot him; I didn't ask him; the only thing I could think of was—help for him."

There was a rather long pause. The inspector smoked quietly, watching her in complete silence for a moment. She found herself tracing the outline of the largest stain on the desk top. It had a fantastic look of a man's face, round and jocular, seen in profile. She wrenched her gaze from it and met Friker's eyes.

He said, "How long was it before he died?"

"A moment or two. Perhaps longer. I couldn't possibly say."

"Yet the three people in the house, who heard the shots and came at once, did not enter."

"No."

He looked impatient and a little contemptuous. "Don't try to deny that that door over there, leading into the main hall, and thus the rest of the house, was locked. Otherwise they would have been here, too. And would have heard what your husband—actually said. And would have seen what you did."

"I've told you . . ."

"Begin again, please," he said abruptly. "You heard the shots . . ."

Elizabeth pushed her hair back from her temples wearily and began again. And then slowly, minutely, prompted by his questions told it all again. And then again. Desperately, telling herself, each time, that there must be no variation—nothing forgotten, nothing uncertain.

Time went on and night gave way to a gray reluctant dawn.

The repetition began to seem endless; the same questions repeated in varying ways began to wear down her guard. And when it had reached a point where it seemed almost unendurable, the inspector gave a low direction to the sub-inspector who began to write her answers as she gave them. She was by that time sitting in the chair where Robert had died and was so near the end of her endurance that it did not seem to matter, and the stains of dried blood there in the light, just before her eyes, were only a part of a whole vicious nightmare.

By that time, too, she was only repeating, over and over again, replies she had made so many, many times.

So the variation in the questions took her by surprise.

Occasionally, during that time, there had been a few words between the inspector and his assistant— low, brief asides of which she was scarcely aware. So she knew nothing of the thing the sub-inspector had found until, finally, Friker rose and came to the desk. And, looking across it, varied his questions. For he said, "Madam, does this belong to you?"

And held a revolver across the desk, holding it carefully in a handkerchief.

She stared at it.

"No!"

"It was found in your bedroom, Madam, hidden behind some books."

"I don't believe it. I can't believe . . ."

"It has recently been fired. Are you ready now to confess?"

She tried to rise. She did rise, clutching at the desk for support.

"No—no—no!" she thought she screamed it, but couldn't have done so for the detective's face seemed curiously far away and uncomprehending. And, as curiously, the floor below her feet seemed to sway— the desk itself moved.

Friker came from a black mist and took her arm.

She was aware of that and she heard her own tired voice saying something—she wasn't sure what. And then she was sitting again in a chair, with the light again pouring into her face. It was so bright and so harsh that she closed her eyes. And sank into a grateful kind of darkness which shut out voices.

From it presently someone was lifting her. She was perfectly aware of that, but the vague, rather confused darkness was so much better than the glaring light on her face that she kept her eyes closed defensively. She was aware, too, but in a rather dim and vague way, that she was being carried out of the room.

Friker's voice faded into the distance. She was put down rather gently on a bed, she thought, and opened her eyes slowly and with a queer kind of difficulty. She was in a guest room. And somebody was saying in a low voice, "Undress her and get her into bed. I'll get something hot for her to drink."

"Yes, sir." That was Marianna.

She roused.

"Marianna . . ."

"Don't talk, Madam. Let me help you."

"But the police . . ."

"They are still here. Madam is to rest."

The maid was quick and skillful. But that grateful, shadowy oblivion had gone and Elizabeth was sharply conscious again when there was a knock at the door and Cyril came in with a cup in his hand. He dismissed the maid and came to sit on the edge of the bed.

"I've brought you some beef broth," he said. "Drink it. You've had no dinner, that's all that's wrong. You'll be all right again as soon as you've had some food."

"Cyril, he believes I did it. They found the revolver . . ."

"Yes, I know." He looked at the cup for a long moment and then said slowly, "He hasn't made a formal charge, Elizabeth. You are not under arrest—" He checked himself so abruptly he might as well have added "—yet." But he said instead, "Drink this while it's hot."

13

"Cyril, I didn't do it."

"I know, Elizabeth. Don't go all to pieces now. Here—drink this." He held the cup to her lips and made her drink it.

"That's better. Now then. You'd better get some sleep now and talk in the morning. It's nearly that now." He started to rise.

"Cyril." She clung to the lapels of his coat. "Wait. I've got to know. What—what is he—the inspector—going to do?"

"I don't know."

"He believes I did it."

"Elizabeth, he suspects everyone."

"But I was alone with Robert. We quarreled. And now the revolver. Friker doesn't believe the truth . . ."

"That's his business, Elizabeth, to suspect."

"He knows about everything . . ."

He interrupted her sharply.

"Everything? What do you mean?"

"He knew about the hall door to the study being locked. He knew we had quarreled; he knew I had packed my bag intending to leave the house and then unpacked. He knew everything."

He looked at her thoughtfully for a moment. "I was afraid of that," he said. "Well. We'll have to go on from there. Look, Elizabeth, I'm not going to let you talk now."

"I can't sleep . . ."

"Oh, yes, you can. You must. Remember this. It's been only a few hours since he was murdered; there'll be other evidence and it can't, all of it, point toward you. And as to the revolver, so far it's only their guess that it was the revolver that was used to kill Robert. There are all sorts of tests—ballistics, fingerprints . . ." A sharp alarm touched his face and he said quickly, "You didn't happen to touch the revolver, did you?"

"No! No, never. I never saw it before. I didn't know it was there. Cyril . . ."

"I believe you, Elizabeth. Well, then it can't show your fingerprints. And they can't prove your possession of it. Remember that. And remember, too—*you didn't do it*. Truth does have a certain force and weight of its own."

"Not if he doesn't use it."

"Well, there's one thing he can't fail to see. The front door was open when I came. He can't get around that. And no one remembers, or at least admits having opened it. Dyke was outdoors shortly before, but he says he closed the door when he came in. None of the servants remembers opening it; Flemming, who seems to be pinch-hitting for Leech, insists that it was closed and locked with a night latch as always at ten o'clock. So there you are. Somebody—anybody—could have entered the house. How he got in and out of the study is something else."

There was a kind of hesitancy in his voice which was like a question. She said, "What are you thinking? Tell me."

"All right. I will. Elizabeth—you aren't shielding anyone, are you?"

"No, Cyril."

He was looking at her very gravely, searching her eyes as if to discover in them something beyond her words.

"Because—well, you see, Elizabeth, the only way that I see now for anyone to escape would be through your suite. And while it's possible, I suppose, that anyone gifted with almost incredible speed could have shot him, unlocked the door to your rooms, run through the hall past your dressing room, and through your bedroom and so, by way of the balcony, made an escape, it—well, the speed is too incredible. Even allowing for those few seconds after the sound of the shots when, you say, you didn't move. You would certainly have heard something. Did you?"

"No."

He waited a moment, as if to allow her to talk, and

as she didn't, he went on, even more soberly, "And it isn't only the speed of it that is against such a theory. For you see, no one knowing you were in your rooms would have taken such a risk. That's the important thing. No one would have taken such a risk unless—I hate to say it, Elizabeth; it's what the inspector thinks so we've got to face it—unless that person knew you would shield him. Do you see? With the inspector and on the basis he now has, it lies between you and some-one you—are protecting. You mustn't think of doing that, you know. No matter how great an appeal to your—your loyalty or your sense of—oh, of anything. I mean," said Cyril carefully, "if someone killed him in order to protect you, still it would be wrong for you to take the burden of it."

But Dyke had an alibi. Therefore he hadn't killed Robert to protect her, or for any other reason. She sat up straight in bed and put both her hands upon his. "Cyril, I'm not protecting anyone. I would tell you the truth. I have told you the truth."

Again he looked searchingly into her eyes for a moment. Then he patted her hands briskly and got up. "All right. That's all I wanted to know. Go to sleep."

"But, Cyril . . ."

"I'll pull the curtains tight. Sleep as late as you can."

"But I can't . . ."

"Oh, yes, you can," he said again and pulled the curtains close across the open jalousies to keep out the

107

faint dawning light, and went away, closing her door firmly behind him.

But there were so many things he hadn't said. He hadn't said that someone close to them, someone in the house must have murdered Robert Dakin.

Her mind was going in weary circles, staggering along as if it had a dizzy, exhausted and clumsy body. How long would it be before they charged her with murder? The last thing she thought, however, before she did actually fall into a heavy sleep was perfectly clear.

There were, in fact, two things. Cyril hadn't thought to tell her how it was that he happened along at just the time when she—when they all—needed him. Not that it mattered.

The other was obscurely puzzling. That, too, was an omission, but a different kind of omission, and it was the monkeys. The curious, worn and shabby little wooden image they had found on Robert's desk, below his dead and helpless hands. It was queer that the inspector had not asked her about the monkeys. He had asked about everything else.

Her thoughts kept circling about the little wooden image—so oddly out of place, bizarre on that blood-stained desk, below a murdered man's hands.

She was certain she had never seen it before.

Outside dawn turned abruptly from gray to gold.

Ting-ting birds and wild canaries sang gently in the trees around the villa; scarlet hibiscus and white angel trumpets opened wider to the morning sun; dew sparkled softly on the grass—quite as if, during the black night hours just past, murder had not walked into that long, old house, vine covered, its graveled walks and tiled terrace warming now in the sun.

The house, however, felt it. It was in its silence—a waiting, listening silence that, to Elizabeth, was never to leave it.

She felt it first when she awoke, late that morning, and lay there, remembering all in a flood the horror the night had held. The horror and the danger. The house was hushed and silent. Perfectly aware of what had happened, she thought all at once, and watchful. Waiting.

There must be people about. Ruth—Dyke—the police. But, just then, the silence was like a spell. She had to force herself at last to ring the bell for her maid.

Marianna, bringing her usual breakfast tray, had little, if any, news. There were police about the house, she said; Leech was still unconscious and the doctor had sent a nurse—a man—to take care of him. (*A policeman* thought Elizabeth; *posted to listen to the servants' conversation and pick up any stray grains of information?*)

By this time telegraph wires and cables were busy. She thought of newspapers in New York and London and tried not to think of them and told Marianna to bring her clothes. Her own suite was still locked by the police, Marianna told her, but presently returned with a white thin dress, simply tailored and cool.

She was very pale. She saw herself in the mirror; almost as white as her white dress, with shadows under her eyes. Well, she couldn't hide in her room like an ostrich with its head in the sand. But when she turned to leave it, again she had almost to force herself to do so.

She went slowly downstairs. There were two policemen in the hall, dignified in their spotless white jackets and observant. They looked at her but said nothing.

And Dyke opened the library door, saw her and said, "Elizabeth," quickly and eagerly and then checked himself with a side glance at the two policemen. "Will you come in," he added more distantly. "There are some things for you to see." She went into the library and he closed the door. He said, "Elizabeth, oh, my darling . . ." No one else was in the library. He took her hands and kissed them and said, "I had to see you. I couldn't wait. They mustn't see us together, of course. All they want is a motive. Oh, my darling." He put his arms around her, drawing her close to him. "Listen, Elizabeth," he said, "I thought it best last night not to let anyone guess—especially Charlie Hawes—exactly how things stood between us. It—it's a nasty situation, Elizabeth. All the inspector needs is a hard and fast motive. It would go—badly with you, my darling, if he got a hint about us."

She drew back against his arms, but he would not release her. "But, Dyke—I never meant . . ."

"Elizabeth, there's something else I want you to understand. I didn't kill Uncle Bob. Do you believe me?"

His eyes were bright and dark and compelling, intensely personal and animated. Not at all like the inspector's eyes, she thought irrelevantly.

Dyke went on, "I have an alibi, you know. Charlie and I were having a drink there in the dining room when we heard the shots. It's a perfectly hard and fast alibi."

"Yes, I—I know."

"I only wish, you poor darling," said Dyke, "that you had as good a one. Elizabeth, I—I would have done anything to help you last night. I mean, when Uncle Bob dragged you upstairs. But there wasn't anything I could do. I would only have made a bad matter worse. There was no sense in trying to reason with him; he didn't know what he was doing. And I didn't think he would hurt you. I didn't want to arouse him to—to worse brutality. You do understand, don't you, my darling?"

"Yes—yes, I understand."

"I love you so, dear. I would do anything in the world for you. I wish I had no alibi. I wish I could tell them I did it—anything to save you."

"Then you know about . . ."

"About the revolver? Yes. But don't worry about that, Elizabeth. They'll never be able to trace it to you. You never saw it before, Cyril says."

"That's true."

"Don't pull away from me, Elizabeth; let me hold you just a moment in my arms."

"Please, Dyke. I—I'm very tired."

Instantly he made her sit in a lounge chair. He opened the jalousies at the eastern windows so the soft morning air flooded the room, and sunlight, barred by the wide green slats, lay upon the darkly polished floor. He pulled a footstool to her chair and sat there looking up at her, and taking her hands again in his own.

"Elizabeth, they say the only way of escape was through your suite. Are you sure there was no one . . ."

"I saw no one, Dyke. I heard nothing but the shots."

"I know it's hard to talk of it. After that horrible inquiry last night. But—but, Elizabeth, tell me. No one can hear and I won't tell a soul. Who shot him? I mean—tell me, darling, for your own protection. I want to help you. But I have to know . . ."

"But, Dyke, I don't know who shot him. If I knew I would tell the inspector."

"You can trust me, you know, dear."

"Dyke, I don't know who did it. Please believe me."

Again he waited a moment, staring at her, smiling a little, patting her hands softly. "Darling, you mean you won't tell me. Uncle Bob told you before he died. You know he did. It isn't possible that he wouldn't tell you."

"He didn't. You'll have to believe me. I'm telling you the truth."

"Don't be angry, darling. I only ask because I—I want to protect you. That's the reason. I won't have you sacrificing yourself—refusing to tell Friker—letting him arrest you—don't you understand?"

"I don't feel," said Elizabeth wearily, "as if I should ever understand anything again. Please . . ."

"Darling, I've got to ask you one or two things. I'm sorry but—I've got to. Have you told anyone about the helium?"

"Helium!"

"Does Friker know of it?"

"No. That is, he didn't ask me about it. What do you mean?"

"Does—this Englishman know? Cyril? Did you tell him?"

She thought back. And rather suddenly remembered a clear little scene at a dinner table. "Yes, he knows," she said slowly. "Robert told him."

"I see. Anyone else?"

"I don't think so. Charlie . . ."

"Oh, Charlie, of course. He knows everything." He was frowning now, thoughtfully. "Elizabeth, don't tell anyone else. It has nothing to do with Uncle Bob's murder. And the less said of it the better. Understand?"

She didn't. But if it had nothing to do with Robert's death, then it was not important. She nodded.

And Dyke said softly, "It's queer, isn't it, Elizabeth? I was thinking of your letter to me. Your poor, frightened little letter. There's one phrase, one expression you used; you said, I remember—'I don't know what to do but I must do something; anything to end it.' " He stopped for a moment. And then said again, " 'Anything to end it.' Darling, don't look so white and sick and frightened! It's safe with me! Friker will never know."

Could she have said that? But she could, she could have said anything in that frantic—that horribly impulsive and unwise letter.

"No one will know," cried Dyke again. "Why, it would be absolutely fatal with the inspector—that is —oh, I don't mean that, darling. Forgive me, dear; it's only because I love you so much. He'll never know; no one will know. Don't think of it again." He had her hands again, kissing them, holding them to his face, protesting, when the library door opened and Cyril walked in, saw them and stopped short. Then rather quickly his hand went out to close the door behind him.

14

"SORRY," HE SAID, coming forward. "There are people in the hall."

Dyke released Elizabeth's hand but did not move. Cyril said, "I didn't know you were down, Elizabeth. I didn't mean to interrupt."

"That's all right," said Dyke quickly. "We were only talking. How's everything going, Kirby? Is there anything new?"

Cyril did not reply but instead spoke to Elizabeth. "Sleep any?"

"Yes. Cyril, have they found out whether it was the revolver . . ."

"I don't know. It's early yet. Remember, it hasn't been long, really—it may take days to gather and sift all the evidence."

"It seems—months since last night," said Elizabeth, looking back as if across a great and terrible gulf.

Cyril said, "Charlie Hawes says Friker asked him for a lot of information about Major Dakin's business."

"Why didn't he ask me?" asked Dyke.

Cyril glanced at him briefly and then looked back at Elizabeth. There was, and had been since his abrupt entrance, a faint and indefinable change in his manner. It was slight, almost imperceptible, yet present like a little chill in the air. He explained rather tersely, "Names of banks, clubs, business associates, friends—all that kind of thing. He supplied everything he could supply. Had to, of course. It was all right, wasn't it?"

"I'm not so sure—" began Dyke.

"Yes, of course," said Elizabeth. "Cyril, I'm so glad you didn't go back to your yacht. It's good of you to stay on." He must intend to stay, for she noted briefly that he had changed from the dinner jacket of the previous night to whites—the uniform of the tropics. Therefore he must have sent to his yacht for clothes.

Dyke said quickly, "He can't help staying. Don't flatter yourself, Elizabeth, that he's doing it altogether out of the kindness of his heart. You see, he's a suspect, too."

"Is that . . ."

Cyril nodded shortly. "It's quite true. That is, Friker merely indicated that he would appreciate my staying on here for a day or two. He had no right to demand it, of course. But one doesn't go against a polite indication of exactly that nature. I thought you wouldn't mind."

"Mind!" cried Elizabeth. "I can't thank you enough, Cyril."

His gray eyes warmed a little and at once he seemed more like himself.

Dyke, still on the footstool, put his arms boyishly around his knees and looked up speculatively at Cyril.

"I suppose you are included in the list of suspects because of your very opportune arrival last night." He said it very pleasantly, with his usual air of boyish impetuousness. "You did turn up, you know, Kirby, rather promptly at the scene of the crime."

Cyril said to Elizabeth, "If I'm interrupting . . ."

"You are not. Don't go."

He sat down and looked at Dyke. "True again. I did turn up at the time of the murder or shortly after. However, I didn't murder him."

Dyke looked shocked. "Why, Kirby, my dear chap, I had no idea of suggesting . . ."

"I had no idea that you were suggesting that I murdered Major Dakin," said Cyril. "I merely made a statement that happens to be true."

"Well—well, of course," said Dyke. "Too bad you happened along just then. Too bad to involve you in this very unpleasant affair."

Cyril did not speak for a moment. Then he took out cigarettes, quietly offered them to Dyke and Elizabeth and held a match for her, carefully and quite deliberately.

"It's bad for all of us," he said then. "I feel sure that Elizabeth will be cleared, however. It's only the peculiar circumstances of the thing that have stacked up against her. It may take time to prove and disprove; it's not been twenty-four hours yet; some murder cases go on for weeks. So keep your chin up, Elizabeth. You were looking pretty white and shaky when I came in just now. Had anything happened to upset you that I don't know about?"

Dyke shot a warning glance at Elizabeth and said quickly, "We can count on Elizabeth, Kirby. She's got all kinds of courage."

"I'm sure she has," said Cyril. "You didn't answer my question, Elizabeth."

She could feel Dyke's remonstrance almost as if he had spoken to her, warning her not to tell Cyril, not to tell anyone of the letter she had written Dyke on that unlucky day six weeks ago. But it would do no harm; it was cowardly, of course, but it would actually have sustained her just then, she felt, to tell Cyril about it—to listen to his cheerful, sensible reassurances. He would tell her everyone said things like that and didn't mean that they intended to murder anyone. He would tell her that everyone, now and then, had moments of despair.

And, still hesitating because of that silent warning Dyke somehow managed to convey in his very stillness and silence, she did not speak and the door opened again and Flemming said, "Excuse me, Madam . . ."

"Yes, Flemming. What is it?"

"It—it's Madam—I mean Mrs. Dakin, Madam. Mrs. —the other Mrs. Dakin." Flemming's long, lantern-jawed face was disconcerted and nervous. "She is here and she would like to see you."

Charmian!

Dyke got quickly to his feet.

"I'd see her if I were you, Elizabeth," he said. "Show her in, Flemming."

Cyril said—so quietly that it was curious how his voice carried and how quickly Flemming, half way out of the room, stopped—"Flemming! Wait a moment." He looked at Elizabeth. "Don't see her unless you're up to it, Elizabeth. She has no right to call just now; you're not obliged to see her."

"You're quite right, of course," said another voice from the doorway. Flemming, startled, whirled around, almost upsetting Charmian, who stood there. She avoided the confused servant neatly and came into the room. She was not without dignity and seemed to be perfectly aware of her intrusion. "I'm sorry," she said and it sounded sincere. "I had to come." She looked at Elizabeth and then as Dyke advanced she put out her arms. "Dyke!" she exclaimed. "I didn't know you were here."

He kissed her rather perfunctorily.

Cyril had risen, and came to stand at Elizabeth's side.

Dyke said, "How are you, Charmian?"

"I had to come," Charmian said again, looking at Elizabeth.

"Won't you sit down," said Elizabeth. She looked at Flemming, and nodded his dismissal. The door closed and Elizabeth said, "I don't believe you know —may I present Mr. Cyril Kirby? Cyril, this is Robert's first wife, Mrs. Dakin."

Dyke pulled up a chair for Charmian who smiled briefly and spoke to Cyril, and thanked Dyke. Cyril's hand touched Elizabeth's hand lightly, like a promise of support.

Charmian sat back gracefully in her chair; she refused a cigarette Dyke offered and looked again at Elizabeth as if considering exactly how to say whatever it was that she had come to say. She was perfectly composed but looked as if that composure was merely a matter of will. In her simple but extremely smart and cool-looking black-and-white print and large black hat, she looked very much older than she had looked under artificial lights and dressed for the evening. Her thin, lined face was almost haggard under her careful but not elaborate make-up; her white gloved hands gripped her large flat handbag tightly. And she said with an air of resolution that she had an unusual request to make.

"I heard about Robert's—death—early this morning. The police—the inspector, in fact, came to my house very early this morning to tell me about it and to ask me a number of questions. I answered him to the best of my ability, but since I haven't seen or spoken to Robert for over three years, I'm afraid I wasn't very helpful. But—please forgive me for intruding personal matters just now. It's only because certain matters concerning the estate naturally arise at once. Certain questions, I mean, that affect me."

She paused. Cyril did not move or—which was not like him—did not offer to withdraw from what was to be, obviously, a family discussion. Elizabeth waited, too, without speaking.

Dyke, leaning on the mantel, said, "Well, Charmian dear. What's the trouble?"

She seemed almost grateful to him for the word. She said quickly, "That's it exactly. Trouble. I'm afraid I—well, you see, it's money."

"Money," cried Elizabeth in involuntary surprise.

Charmian replied instantly. "Yes. Robert gave me, as you must know, a"—she hesitated and just for an instant, again something unfriendly, queerly spiteful came like a spark into her large green eyes and vanished as quickly—"a very generous alimony," she concluded in a perfectly pleasant and dignified way. "But it stops at his death. And I—I have been extravagant, I know, but I am not here to excuse myself. The fact is"—she stopped and took a quick breath—"the fact is, I have no money. I can't keep up the house I've leased; I can't pay my servants; I can't—I came here, Elizabeth," she said directly, "to ask if you would permit me to stay here for a time. At the villa. Until things have been adjusted. Until I know—what will be done."

It took Elizabeth by surprise, elaborate as had been Charmian's peroration.

Dyke said promptly, "Don't worry about money,

Charmian. We'll see that you have anything you want. Don't give up your house right away. Wait a while until things . . ." He stopped as she turned and looked at him fully.

"It's a very small thing I am asking, Dyke," she said. "Perhaps I have a—feeling about it all. This was my home, you know, for some time. I was Robert's wife for twenty-three years." Dyke's face flushed a little as he met her look and he said nothing. She turned back to Elizabeth. "Forgive me for saying these things. It is not an easy situation for any of us. I don't know anything about Robert's arrangements for his estate, his will, I mean. But I do know that I am very likely to be altogether without an income; every day that I keep up a rather expensive establishment adds to my debts."

"I will pay for that," said Elizabeth. "That is," she added quickly to assuage the other woman's pride, "I will loan you any amount of money you need."

Again a little unfriendly spark glimmered way back in Charmian's eyes. She said, "Thank you. But I can't—I'm afraid I can't explain my feeling to you. I don't ask charity on the part of Robert's—wife. Or his heir," she added, glancing at Dyke who stared at the carpet and still said nothing. "Very well. I'm sorry I troubled you. I only meant to stay until the question of the estate is settled when I will know just what to do. I don't mean that I expect any substantial settlement. Bob told me that he would leave me nothing— that was in our agreement when the alimony was agreed upon. I only hope that out of it all I may find an answer to my own problem. You see, I am being perfectly frank with you. And I am in immediate trouble."

Elizabeth said, "Robert must have provided for you in his will. I'm afraid I haven't had time to think of such things yet. Won't you let me advance you . . ."

"No, thank you," said Charmian definitely. She rose and put out her hand toward Elizabeth. The fingers of the two women touched and parted. "Thank you, too, for letting me see you. I—I really am sorry that things are as they are. It must be rather horrible for all of you. Have the police any kind of clues? The inspector was so evasive with me, I could get nothing from him. Is it true that no one knows who killed Robert?"

"Too true," said Dyke. He laughed ruefully. "You'd better stay away from here, Charmian. Even Cyril is suspected."

"Cyril," said Charmian. "Oh, Mr. Kirby." She turned toward Cyril and their eyes met steadily; Charmian's were unperturbed in their green depths. She smiled very faintly, and politely said, "Good-by, Elizabeth. I'm sorry I have intruded. Only necessity would have induced me to come. Dyke, will you come to my car with me?"

"Oh, certainly," said Dyke quickly. "Certainly."

Perplexed, Elizabeth watched them go. It was asking too much of magnanimity; yet she felt as if she had gone out of her way to make things difficult for Charmian. She looked up at Cyril.

"Cyril, what ought I have done?"

"Had her here," said Cyril promptly.

"Do you mean . . ."

"Certainly. Shall I go and tell her?"

"But if it's money, as she says . . ."

"It probably isn't," said Cyril. "And I'd awfully like to know what her real motive is."

15

CHARMIAN, still in the hall with Dyke, accepted Elizabeth's capitulation with unruffled composure and a minimum of gratitude but returned, nevertheless, shortly after lunch, having left a maid to pack. It did not occur to Elizabeth until later that Charmian's presence in the house would oblige her to move back to her own suite, for the supply of guest rooms was not unlimited and Charmian would have to have the room in which Elizabeth had taken refuge.

Charmian, however, went away then, Dyke putting her in the car that, with its Negro driver, was waiting.

The sun was bright on the softly colored tiles of the terrace; it was queer, thought Elizabeth, that so little sun entered the house. Reluctant to return just then to the shadowy and too spacious house, she went to sit on the wide balustrade that bordered the terrace. Pots of tropical flowers, all brilliant bloom and thick green foliage, were interspersed with deep wicker chairs, and the sun poured down over all. Cyril went with her.

"What is her motive, then?" said Elizabeth, watching Charmian's car wind down the drive to the great stone gates and disappear.

"I don't know. Perhaps none. It's only that—well, you know, straws show the way the wind blows. The fact is, Elizabeth, we are in a tough spot."

"I am, you mean."

"I mean all of us. And we need every ounce of . . ."

He broke off as Dyke came up the steps, and said quickly, "Elizabeth, before Dyke gets here—that revolver. What kind was it, do you know?"

"It was small—square-looking—I haven't any idea what make it was. I'm sorry, Cyril. But I don't know any more than that."

"Perhaps it belonged to Dakin."

"I never saw it before. I don't know whether he had one or not."

"Mind if I join you?" said Dyke and sat down beside Elizabeth on the balustrade. "Funny," he said, "how bright it is outdoors and how"—he shrugged his shoulders as if shaking off a weight—"how gloomy it is in the house." He glanced up along the front of the house. "There seem to be windows enough, too. It's just something about the house. Those directly above are Uncle Bob's study windows, aren't they?"

All three looked up.

"Directly above?" said Elizabeth. "No, those are my dressing-room windows. The study windows are further along; at the end of the terrace. Ruth's windows are next—just above the place where the terrace ends and the grass begins."

"Oh. I see," said Dyke. "I'd forgotten how it was."

Cyril got up, walked over to the grass below Ruth's windows and stared down at the green turf thoughtfully. And Dyke said in a low voice, "Elizabeth, don't trust this fellow Kirby too much. Don't tell him anything. I'll tell you why later . . ."

Cyril came strolling back toward them.

And Dyke went on quickly, "See here, Kirby. Isn't there something we can do? I mean it seems so silly just to do nothing and wait for Friker to turn up evidence against us. Isn't there something we can do to—to protect ourselves?"

"Well, yes," said Cyril unexpectedly. "You can persuade Ruth to take a different attitude."

"Toward . . ."

"Toward Elizabeth, naturally. Ruth may not realize the seriousness of Elizabeth's position. Certainly I don't believe that she really thinks Elizabeth shot him. But she did accuse her."

"That was only in the—the heat of the moment," said Dyke hurriedly. "She wouldn't tell Friker Elizabeth shot him."

"I'm not so sure," said Cyril. He looked reflectively across the green lawn and then up at Ruth's windows. "Ruth hates Elizabeth, you know."

"Hates *me?*" cried Elizabeth. "But she—I scarcely know her. I never saw her until she came here two days ago."

"It doesn't take long to hate," said Cyril rather dryly. "You agree with me, don't you, Dyke?"

Dyke looked uncomfortable.

"Well—of course, Ruth is a law unto herself. Always has been. But she wouldn't give evidence against Elizabeth. She wouldn't do that."

"Not, at any rate, if you stop her, Dyke," said Cyril.

"Stop her! How? She's much more likely to stop me."

"You forget," said Cyril, "that you are your uncle's heir. Aren't you?"

"Well—he—he always said I was to be his heir. That's why he trained me in his business. It's always been understood. Of course, I expect Elizabeth will share in his estate. His wife, you know. And, by the way, Elizabeth, I think it was swell of you to let Charmian come; after all, she is in a difficult position. I happen to know that at the time of their divorce and in order to get the amount of alimony she thought she ought to have—twenty-five thousand a year, Kirby; no small sum—she was given to understand that she would inherit nothing in case Uncle Bob predeceased her. So you see, since her alimony automatically stops, she really is out on a limb. Of course," added Dyke, "I'll see she's taken care of if necessary. But until the estate is settled—" He stopped rather abruptly, looking curiously at Elizabeth. "How did you happen to change your mind?"

Cyril spoke so casually that it didn't appear to check her own explanation, as in fact it did. "Second

128

thought," he said. "Let's decide on something to spike Ruth's guns. I don't mean to insist too much, Dyke, but Ruth strikes me as being a very able and determined and"—he hesitated and said, his quiet, English voice almost apologetic—not to Ruth, but to the use of the melodramatic word—"and relentless woman. A dangerous enemy, in other words."

Elizabeth thought of Ruth's black and white beauty, and the unfathomable depths of her dark eyes. Relentless.

Dyke smoked a moment and said, "But what can I do?"

"As I say, you stand to inherit the business. You must have some influence with Ruth; the business is part of her life, and an important part."

"Oh, I see. You mean bring pressure like that to bear upon Ruth." He shook his head. "The shoe's on the other foot. That is," he caught himself quickly, "I don't mean I can't handle the business—I can; in fact, there are several changes I intend to make. But—well, Ruth *is* efficient you know, and used to the business."

"I see. I didn't ask you to appeal to her sympathy."

"That's no good either," said Dyke promptly. "Ruth—well, it stands to reason she wouldn't be exactly fond of Elizabeth. Especially if she thinks Elizabeth shot him."

"That's exactly the point, Dyke. You must persuade her that she's wrong. You must show her that Elizabeth didn't kill Dakin."

"Glad to try it," said Dyke agreeably. "I'll do what I can."

"But I haven't injured Ruth. I never even knew of her until she came—perhaps I'd heard Robert mention her; that's all. Do you mean"—Elizabeth groped through half-meanings, implications—"do you mean on account of Robert? That she resented my position as his—his wife?"

There was a little silence. Then Dyke said slowly, "Ruth's all right. Got her own notions perhaps. I'll talk to her. Look here, Kirby, do you know anything about the gun they found? Did it belong to Uncle Bob?"

"I don't know. Elizabeth says she doesn't know."

"I suppose it'll take time to trace it. Unless it did belong to Uncle Bob and somebody—Leech or somebody—recognized it. But they can't question Leech till he's conscious."

"There's nothing to do but sit tight," said Cyril. "And wait. But do what you can with Ruth. And I think we'd better get hold of a lawyer for Elizabeth."

"A lawyer!" said Dyke. "What could he do?"

"We could put the case up to him. We'd be prepared in case—well, in case of anything." He didn't say, thought Elizabeth quickly, in case of her arrest with a murder charge.

"New York's a long way off," said Dyke.

"By plane? Only a matter of hours. But there are lawyers nearer. I know a chap in Kingston. Shall I get him?"

"Yes," said Elizabeth.

"Wait a minute, Elizabeth. You don't know—sorry, Kirby, but I have to protect Elizabeth, you know—you don't know anything about this fellow. Don't do anything you'll regret. I advise you to wait; chances are the thing will all blow over for lack of conclusive evidence. If they'd had evidence sufficient to arrest you for murder they'd have done it last night. Right away. Don't forget that. My advice would be to wait; if you have to later, we'll get the best criminal lawyer in the world," said Dyke. "We'll bring on New York lawyers."

Cyril said, "I don't want to over-influence you, Elizabeth. Do as you think best. Wait till tomorrow. Decide then. By that time—something may have happened to clear you."

"That's right," said Dyke quickly. "Wait . . ." The sound of a car coming along the drive interrupted him.

It was, again, the inspector.

Elizabeth's heart sank as she watched him swing up the steps and along the terrace toward them.

"Madam," he said and bowed. He did not smile; his eyes were hard and bright and wholly unrevealing. He went on in a businesslike way. He would be greatly obliged if Madam would not make any attempt to leave the grounds for a time.

"I am not going to escape," said Elizabeth stiffly. "Don't be afraid of that."

"I am not at all afraid that you will escape," said

131

Mr. Friker and bowed again and went into the house.

Charlie Hawes, coming out of the house at the same moment, almost collided with him, ducked out of the way in the nick of time and came toward them.

"I don't like that man," said Charlie gloomily. "Every time I see him I think of hangings. Nasty custom," said Charlie, and wiped his forehead with his handkerchief.

There was, as Cyril had said, nothing they could do but wait. They definitely preferred to linger on the terrace, rather than inside the house with its pall of silence and gloom. Planned and built of stone to resist at the same time termites, sunshine and heat, it was in the latter instances too successful. Its enormous rooms and high ceilings, its polished dark woods and light walls, its cool shadows were also remarkably cheerless.

Ruth did not come downstairs until dinner time. Charmian arrived shortly after lunch—which was a rather dreadful meal, served in the dusky dining room with Flemming's footsteps particularly noiseless on the light rugs and the room extraordinarily silent, as if it was aware of the absence of Robert's great voice—so silent that the little clatter of a knife against a plate sounded loud and sharp.

The afternoon wore on slowly with every dragging moment one of uneasy expectancy. But Friker did not come near her, and the police whom she observed here and there about the grounds all appeared to be busy about concerns of their own. There was no way of knowing what they accomplished or did not accom-

132

plish. There was no way of knowing what the inspector thought or felt, or discovered or didn't discover.

It was a strange and rather horrible day; Elizabeth began desperately to hope that whatever happened would happen soon. But late afternoon came; the sun dropped closer and closer to the green ridge of hills behind the house, leaving the eastern terrace in cool shade. The sea and sky began to turn purple again, and she still didn't know what Friker intended to do—when he would arrest her—what their conclusions or their evidence were after that day of investigation.

It was just before dinner that Cyril urged her to take a walk with him. Dyke and Charmian were in the morning room; Ruth still had not appeared or, if she had, Elizabeth had not seen her.

"We can't go off the place," Cyril said, "but that's all right. You need a little exercise. Come along."

She thought that perhaps the police had gone, but when they crossed the hall and came out the door she found she was mistaken. A figure in white tunic and white helmet walked quietly around from the back of the house. Another emerged, quietly too, from the tall shrubs massed below the balcony. But they had finished with Robert's study and with her own suite. She knew that, for Flemming had inquired, and then had the rooms cleaned and restored to their usual order.

"Let's go down to the garden," said Cyril and led her along the graveled walk, between thick croton hedges, all yellow and orange, to the steps leading down to the garden. No one was there. The beds lay in their formal, peaceful order, curiously, thought Elizabeth, unchanged. But that was absurd of course; the sky didn't change its color nor the sun its course because of human catastrophe; you only felt that everything was different.

They walked up and down the paths quickly, Cyril setting a good, brisk English pace. They had stopped at the oval rosebed to look at the buds, their colors softened by the increasing dusk, when Cyril, holding a bud in his fingers, said an unexpected thing. "Elizabeth, there's something I want to tell you. I would wait in—in other circumstances. But I want you to know it now. I—the fact is, I love you. And if you will —some time, I want you to marry me."

16

THE SOFT purple dusk seemed to draw close like a kind and gentle barrier shutting out the rest of the world. Enclosing Elizabeth and the man beside her and the rose in his hand in a tranquil yet deeply significant world of their own.

Almost as if nothing outside was important.

In the silence she could hear her own heart thudding away briskly—happily, she thought, with a kind of start. And remembered all at once, without desiring to do so, a moment of twilight in the gardens of the hotel at Montego Bay, on the walk above the black sea. Cyril had kissed her lightly, briefly; and then all at once held her and kissed her again. And that kiss had been so very different.

But then they had turned away from that unexpected embrace; they had walked back, rather quickly, to the lights of the hotel.

"Cyril," she began and turned to him, but he was looking at the bud in his hand and he said rather quickly, "I don't want an answer now, Elizabeth. It—wouldn't be fair. I only want you to know what I've told you. You see—I've got to go home. I heard today. I've been called up. I've got to take the first boat I can get."

"Cyril—when?"

He looked at her quickly and away again.

"I don't know. I've talked to Kingston—there's a naval station there. But passenger boats are uncertain. I hope it won't be until—you've been cleared. I want to see you through this. But in any case I wanted you to know that I love you. That's all."

He pulled off the bud and turned around to face her, but did not meet her eyes. Instead he fastened the bud quickly at the throat of her white dress and said rather brusquely, "Well. It's nearly dinner time; shall we go back to the house?"

She had known, of course, that he'd been expecting it. She'd known, when it came, it would come suddenly, and urgently. But she hadn't known that the definite fact of his departure—for England, for war—would fall queerly, like a weight, in her heart.

"Where will you be?" she asked a little huskily.

He shrugged. "I don't know. Wherever they send me. I've been lucky getting this much time. When the war's over—" he stopped suddenly. "Queer, how reminiscent this war is of the other one. But it's different, too. I—sometime I'll see you again, Elizabeth."

"Cyril, I want you to know . . ." She stopped, for she remembered Dyke. She had sent for Dyke; she had told him she regretted their quarrel two years and more ago; she had actually fallen in love with him, just from remembering him during those two years of absence. Hadn't she? And if that image she had fallen in love with was not quite like Dyke in the flesh, still it was Dyke. Wasn't it?

Loyalty, constancy, honesty—a whole string of words arose to jibe at her. And Dyke was counting on her. He'd made that evident only that morning.

The fantastic thing was that she quite simply wanted Cyril to take her in his arms and hold her away from everything else in the world. It was, in that quiet moment, in the dusk, with the shapes of flowers veiled in purple, the one thing she wanted.

But that wasn't possible either. And Cyril said abruptly, "Don't try to think now, Elizabeth. About this, I mean. You're in a bad spot; you need help and —and a refuge. But I don't want you that way."

He took her arm and turned her toward the steps as if to end the thing, then and there. And it was just then that a figure, indistinct in the growing dusk, came down the steps hurriedly, peered around and came rapidly toward them. It was Charlie Hawes, already dressed for dinner, narrow face very pale in the dusk.

"Oh," he said breathlessly. "There you are!"

"What is it? What's happened?"

"Oh, n-nothing. That is, I—I'm sure it's nothing. I—I only wanted to tell you—to tell someone—to—but then it can't be anything. It's almost time for dinner. Are you coming to the house?"

Cyril said briskly enough, yet with a tense note in his voice, too, "What do you mean, Charlie? Is Friker going to make an arrest?"

"Oh, it's nothing to do with Friker," said Charlie. "At least," he added wretchedly, "I'm sure I hope not." He ran a finger around his collar and twitched with nervous fingers at his black tie which, indeed, needed attention, for it was wildly askew. A gleam of hope came into his face and he said, "Perhaps it was the inspector, though I never thought of that. Though why he would take it away . . ." His face fell again. "But he couldn't have got into the filing cabinet. I have the only key."

With a swift motion, Cyril took Charlie's narrow shoulders in a tight grip. "Just exactly what do you mean? Tell me. Hurry. What did the inspector take away?"

"Well, I don't think he did," said Charlie. "After all . . ." He glanced at Cyril's tense face and suddenly accelerated his story, "It was my medicine," he said. "You see I—well, I suffer from neuralgia; I always have; I get horrible attacks of it and there's nothing much I can do about them. They're especially bad in a damp climate. So when I came out here I managed to get together—my doctor knew the circumstances and trusted me with it—a large supply of medicine. It's always worse in a damp climate. Well, just now I discovered it's gone. The whole

138

thing. My medicine, I mean. My box of pills. My pain killer."

"Pain killer! What's in it? What is the stuff?"

"That's what I don't know," confessed Charlie miserably. "But it's marked 'poison.' And there's enough to kill a horse."

"Poison!"

He nodded wretchedly. "That's what the doctor said. He said, 'Take care of this, Hawes; there's enough poison in this little box to kill a horse.' That's exactly what he said." He paused momentarily, wrung his hands together and then said in a kind of moan, "And that's not all."

"It's enough," said Cyril. "Wait a minute. When was the box of pills taken? I mean, when did you last see it in your cupboard?"

"This morning," said Charlie definitely. "I'm sure of it. But Kirby, listen. That isn't all."

"Well, what?"

Charlie glanced quickly around them; the sun, as it does in the tropics, had dropped suddenly out of sight, and in the swift purple dusk the outlines of paths and borders had disappeared. They could barely see the steps leading upward out of the walled and hedged garden.

He leaned toward Cyril and whispered, "A revolver's gone, too." And mopped his forehead with his handkerchief.

"A—oh, come Charlie, you can't be suggesting wholesale slaughter!" said Cyril.

"Sh—don't talk so loud! You never know—after all, Kirby, Dakin was murdered only last night. *Somebody* did it. You can't get around that. And I don't care what anybody says, I don't think it was"—his eyes shifted nervously to Elizabeth and back to Cyril —"I don't think it was Mrs. Dakin. No matter what the evidence is against her. So then—who did it? And —and—well there you are. Poison; a gun!"

"*What* gun?" demanded Cyril in a voice of smothered fury. "*Whose* gun? I thought you said there wasn't any . . ."

"No, no, I told the inspector that the gun he found wasn't Major Dakin's, and it wasn't. But I didn't tell him that there was a gun. Major Dakin had had a gun for years; I kept it in the back of my filing cabinet. The steel filing cabinet where I kept his letters and carbon copies and all. I had the key to it; the inspector couldn't get into it and he didn't ask to. At least," he added thoughtfully, "he hasn't asked to yet; I suppose he will."

"Let me get this straight. After you found the medicine was gone . . ."

"I went straight to my room—my workroom, I mean; the little room under the stairs. And I locked the door and then I went and opened the cabinet and the—the gun was gone. Now then, do you believe me when I say something's going on?" His voice rose shrilly and he hushed it quickly, glancing again over his shoulder.

"I didn't know he had a gun," said Elizabeth suddenly. "Charlie, are you sure?"

His hands flapped up and down nervously. "Of course! Saw it every day. Never got it out; never touched it; it's been there for years. I tell you somebody . . ." He drew nearer Cyril. "Listen. Tell me the truth; I won't tell a soul. Didn't Major Dakin tell her"—he indicated Elizabeth but did not address her—"who killed him? I won't tell. But I think you ought to let me know the truth. Just," said Charlie simply, "in order to protect myself."

"Protect yourself from what?"

"From too much of my own medicine," said Charlie with simple sincerity. "Mrs. Dakin, who killed him? Didn't he tell you? In all that time before he died, didn't you ask him?"

"No!" said Cyril. "Positively not. Believe me, Charlie, she knows nothing. Do you understand? Absolutely nothing. Why—why if she knew who killed him, wouldn't she tell the inspector? Think. Wouldn't she tell him to protect herself? Don't be silly."

Charlie's white, rabbity face looked even whiter.

"Maybe she did tell," he said in a low voice, his eyes darting into the shadows around them. "Maybe she did tell. And that's why he didn't arrest her. With all he's got against her."

"Charlie!" Cyril stepped forward so quickly that Charlie jerked back as if to dodge a blow. But Cyril said, "Who says that? Who told you that?"

There was a little silence. Then Charlie said: "No-body. I—nobody. Forget it, Kirby. Let's go into the house. It's time for dinner."

"You've said too much not to say more," said Cyril. But Charlie had turned completely stubborn.

"I tell you nobody said that. I—forget it. All of it."

"Do you want me to tell Friker about your medicine and the gun? He could make a search for them, you know."

"No," said Charlie after a moment. "He'd say just what you think. That I'm scared. And I am. If you're not coming now, I'll go along."

Elizabeth said quietly, "Thank you, Charlie, all the same, for having faith in me. And for warning me."

But Charlie was still stubborn and sulky. "It's all right," he said, and turned and went away, disappearing in the dusk around the steps. And Cyril said suddenly and rather harshly, "The trouble is, he's right. It may mean nothing; it can mean anything—I mean that stupid business of his medicine being gone. And the gun. Probably the gun's been gone for days—weeks even. He's just now noticed it because he was scared and looking for it. Maybe, even, he took it to protect himself and for some reason of his own doesn't want to confess it. Charlie's a funny duck. Always scary. He's got the wind up now. But he's right about the others thinking Dakin must have told you something. That is," said Cyril, his voice queer and tense in the soft twilight, "whoever killed him—

whoever's got a guilty conscience will think that. It—it's not very pleasant, of course. Guilt is one of those things you can't figure on in advance. It's unpredictable."

"Do you mean, Cyril, that *I'm* in danger?"

"Of course not." He turned to her quickly. His voice was instantly and heartily reassuring. Too heartily? "What nonsense! Your only danger is Friker. And given time he'll get at the truth and free you. You do believe that, dear. Don't you? You must believe it."

Perhaps she said yes. She wasn't sure what she said. For there was something queerly disturbing about Charlie Hawes' jerky, half-whispered, wholly perplexing little story.

All the way back to the house she kept thinking of it. Cyril said no more of it, or of the thing Charlie's coming had interrupted.

The trouble was the flavor of truth about it.

The medicine (poison? what?) had certainly vanished and it wasn't likely that in searching the house the police had found and taken it away, for Friker would have inquired about it; he would have questioned Charlie. And anyway—anyway Robert had been shot.

And the gun had certainly vanished for there was conviction in Charlie's voice when he told them of the circumstances. As to that, there had been conviction and real nervousness in his voice and manner during the whole of the unpleasant little interview.

She was relieved to find, later at the dinner table, that Charlie had, by that time, somewhat recovered himself although he ate little and said less and had made quite a mound of little bread pellets beside his plate by the time the meal was over.

And if lunch had been difficult, dinner was worse. For Ruth was there and Charmian, and Flemming in a burst of tact had placed Dyke at Robert's place at the foot of the table, which only emphasized Robert's absence. Absence forever from that room, from that gloomy house, from everything he had known— but not from their lives.

Leech was still unconscious; the nurse sent by the doctor sent word by Flemming that his pulse was irregular but that he was doing as well as could be expected. And a moment later, Flemming inadvertently addressed Charmian as Madam in asking a direction and dropped the bread tray in his subsequent embarrassment.

Ruth looked like a ghost except for her heavily painted lips; apparently she and Charmian had already encountered each other, for when they met at dinner it was without surprise or greeting. Cyril, Dyke and Charmian bore the brunt of the long silences at dinner for they tried to keep up a semblance of conversation. Elizabeth found it an ordeal. She was uneasily conscious of everything; of Charlie's bread pellets, of Cyril's gallant efforts at talk; of Dyke's nervousness at the other end of the table. But she was mainly conscious of Charmian's presence and of Ruth's. Charmian, Ruth and herself.

She thought once, strangely, how Robert Dakin would have laughed if he could have seen them—the three women in his life, gathered together after his death. Because that death was a murder. Because they couldn't separate. But that was fancy. She caught herself toying with a roll, on the very verge of competing with Charlie's growing mound of pellets, and ordered coffee in the library.

It was, actually, a brief meal; and it was after they'd finished coffee that she had her strange interview with Ruth. For Ruth came to her quite directly as she was passing through the hall after having gone to see Leech.

"Elizabeth." How old and haggard Ruth looked, thought Elizabeth; yet she was dressed carefully, in a black dinner gown which set off her white shoulders and breast and her lovely slim figure.

"Yes, Ruth."

"You've been to the kitchen?"

"I went to see Leech. The butler . . ."

"Yes, I know. Elizabeth, will you come out on the terrace a bit? I want to talk to you. Alone."

She hesitated, then turned toward the hall and Ruth followed her. They went quietly outdoors; no one saw them leave, for the others were in the library, still talking in a desultory way over their coffee cups. On the terrace with the Spanish tiles still warm under their slippered feet, the two women strolled to the balustrade and paused.

The night was warm and balmy and heavy with the curiously sweet odor of the tropics. It was a dark night, so the slopes below, the sea and the sky all blended into a warm, soft blackness. Only the lights of Montego Bay, directly across the bay toward the east, gave the night dimension. Elizabeth looked at the twinkling yellow lights and thought fleetingly of the historic old town that lay there, still glowing and alive in the night—of pirates and picaroons and slave revolts, of elegant sugar-estate owners, living like kings in their great houses amid those very hills. And all around the green and gemlike island, with its jagged mountains, its fertile valleys, its swift, short rivers, lay the blue Caribbean. The Spanish Main— blue and gold and treacherous. She thought of Port Royal, that pirate's city, wicked and rich and glittering, sunk long since in those blue waves so all that remained was, when the tide was low, a church steeple pointing upward. A commentary if you wished.

Two hundred and fifty years ago, that was. And now Montego Bay was a winter resort, gay and glamorous, patronized by royalty and movie stars and wealth but never forgetting its rich and somber memories.

For an instant she had escaped the present. It was a wrench to come back, inexorably to herself. Ruth, silent, too, and thoughtful, moved at last. She took a long breath; she opened her lovely, jeweled cigarette case, offered Elizabeth a cigarette and took one herself.

She said without preamble, "I don't like you, Elizabeth. I never liked you. I—I have hated you. I still do."

"But you . . ."

"You see," said Ruth simply, "he married you." Her voice was perfectly hard and controlled.

There was another little silence. It was as if a story told itself briefly. Twenty-five years. Had she loved him all that time? His divorce from Charmian. Freedom. Then abruptly the news of his remarriage. To a young wife.

"Ruth . . ." said Elizabeth unsteadily.

"But that—doesn't matter now. Let me finish. Last night I thought you killed him. Now, I'm—not so sure. Elizabeth, what happened to the monkeys?"

17

"The monkeys! I don't know."

Ruth turned abruptly to face her. Lights came from the drawing-room windows and lay upon the terrace in blocks, and Ruth stood half-in, half-out of one such block, so her black dress blended with the shadow and her white face was full in the light.

"You know what I mean, don't you? That little wooden figure of the three monkeys."

"Yes, of course. I don't know what—or if anything happened to them. Inspector Friker didn't mention them when he questioned me last night."

"Oh. He didn't ask me about them either. Do you—Elizabeth, do you remember seeing them on the desk? I mean after"—the word came out hard, as if she had to force herself to speak it—"after Bob's death? You were in the study a long time with the policemen. You must have noticed. Were the monkeys on the desk then?"

Elizabeth thought back; she could remember only

the blood stains, one of them shaped like the profile of a man, wasn't it? There must have been the usual array of cigarette boxes and ashtrays; ink and pens and blotters. She could only remember the blood stains. But she would have remembered the monkeys if they had been there. She was sure of that. And she had wondered, later, why Friker had not questioned her about them.

"No, I'm sure the monkey figure was not on the desk. I would have remembered."

There was a little pause.

Ruth had turned again so her profile was clear and strong against the night. She watched the twinkling lights across the bay for a moment.

"Queer," she said at last. "Elizabeth"—she didn't look over her shoulder as Charlie had done, but there was the same suggestion of surreptitiousness. Her clear voice lowered and she said, "Elizabeth, who killed him? I'm willing to—to accept the fact that someone else might have done it. At first I was sure it was you; it made twice you had taken him from me—this time forever. You may not understand my love for him. To you, he was—what he was. But there's only one way to understand love," said Ruth in a low voice and paused as if that understanding was more, just then, than she could bear. But in a moment she went on, "Yet now—now I'm not so sure. Oh, I know you say you didn't. Please hear me out. Or rather tell me what he told you."

"Nothing. I didn't ask him. Everyone keeps asking

me that. And he didn't tell me anything. You must believe me."

Ruth used Charlie's very words. She said, "But why, then, haven't they arrested you? With all that evidence against you?"

Elizabeth turned to Ruth and put her hands on Ruth's arms.

"Ruth, I've told you the truth."

"What were you doing, then—all that time before you came to the door and let us come in? Don't you see," cried Ruth, her voice suddenly shaken and harsh, "don't you see I might have been with him when he died."

Elizabeth drew her hands away. "I'm sorry, Ruth," she said. "I'm sorry for everything. But I don't know who killed him. I don't know why the inspector has not yet arrested me. I think he will arrest me tomorrow—or as soon as he gets whatever corroborative evidence he must have. And I don't know anything about the monkeys."

Ruth said abruptly, "Of course, you understand that nothing on earth could make me hate you less. Whether you meant to or not, you took away from me everything that . . ."

The door from the morning room at the other end of the terrace, down near the balcony, opened and closed and a man came toward them. His shirtfront, his face, the red tip of his cigarette, gradually came out of the darkness. It was Dyke. Ruth had stopped speaking as the door opened; when he neared them she said, "I'm going in," and went quickly toward the main entrance from which they had come. Dyke said, "Wasn't that Ruth? What's she in such a hurry for? Well, I'm glad she's gone. I haven't had a chance to talk to you alone since morning."

"Is there any news?" It was always what she thought first.

He shook his head and, standing beside her, put one arm lightly around her waist.

"No, there's no news. I don't know what they're doing. All this waiting is pretty difficult—for us, I mean. I've reached the point where I jump if anybody speaks to me quickly and Charlie Hawes just now flung a cup of coffee at Charmian."

"Charlie did that!"

"Not purposely; I believe somebody turned on the wireless unexpectedly. Charmian had just poured it for him and it went on her. Poor Charmian. I had a talk with her, Elizabeth; I think we ought to do something for her, eventually. That is, if you want to."

"The will . . ."

He shook his head.

"Uncle Bob wasn't one to forgive and forget. I'm almost certain he made no provision for her. However"—he paused for a thoughtful few seconds—"however," he went on in a light tone, "it wouldn't hurt to open the will tomorrow. I believe there's a copy somewhere in the house; at least Charlie thinks so. In the safe, perhaps. Then we'll know where we stand."

"Doesn't the will have to be opened by Robert's lawyer?" asked Elizabeth.

Dyke shrugged. "I suppose that's customary," he said. "But if you and I agree to open and take a look at it I don't know who's going to stop us. And anyway, the lawyer being in the States and circumstances being as they are, I don't imagine the police will stand on ceremony. I don't object to the will being opened and read, and I don't suppose you object and since presumably we are the heirs—well, as I said, I don't know who's going to stop us. Do you object?"

"N-no," said Elizabeth slowly.

"Besides," said Dyke, "his lawyer's got a copy of it; you can rest assured of that. And if everybody is standing by when the safe is opened and the will read there's no chance of any hocus-pocus. I mean, your interests are protected."

"I wasn't thinking of that," said Elizabeth. "And I think the police will insist upon seeing the will; I don't object to that. But, Dyke, why did Charmian come here? What does she want?"

Again there was a little pause. He flicked ashes from his cigarette carefully over the balustrade.

"Well," he said finally, "she really is in a bad situation, you know, but if there was any very special reason for her coming I'd say it was the emeralds."

"Emeralds!"

"She always felt they belonged to her, you know.

They are tremendously valuable, of course, but even so they are more than just jewels to Charmian. They were a career. She hadn't a very happy life; the fact was they married, she and Uncle Bob, to satisfy each other's ambitions. He was on his way up; she—her family rather—was on its way down. He was self-made and lacked social graces; she had a certain position; she knew things he didn't know. He wanted that from her; she wanted a man who was making and would make money. They hit it off until after the boy died; then they took separate ways, as you know. But she loved the emeralds. As you see, she's a woman of great nervous energy; dynamic in an odd way, except she is too emotional for anything that requires a sustained effort. Anyway, the thing is, she loves those emeralds. And she wants them," said Dyke. "But that isn't what I want to talk to you about."

"But if she wants the emeralds why shouldn't she have them?"

"Never mind Charmian. There's something else. Elizabeth, I want you to get rid of that fellow Kirby."

She whirled around in astonishment.

"You can't mean Cyril!"

His arm tightened around her.

"Yes, darling. I do mean Cyril."

"But—but Cyril's all right. He's been everything that's kind and helpful."

"Oh, has he? I know he's given you that impression. He's very clever—especially, I imagine with women. He's been making love to you, hasn't he?"

"Really, Dyke . . ."

"Don't be angry. Listen. Charmian just told me something interesting about him. She's lived here and in England a lot, you know; gossip gets around. He used to be in the British army, you know."

"Yes, I know. He is again. He's been called . . ."

"In the Intelligence Service," said Dyke. "The rumor is that that's still, really, his job. Has been, secretly, all this time."

"But suppose it is," said Elizabeth after a moment. "That doesn't affect us."

"I'm afraid it does, my dear. You see, all the notes and reports about the helium have simply vanished. Into thin air. Friker didn't take them. I had them myself; I had them put away. I didn't see any sense in talking about the helium; it's still a secret until everything is all settled. Anyway, it doesn't exactly belong to us as private individuals, I mean. Uncle Bob gave me the notes to put away just before dinner that night—last night, that was. It seems so long. At any rate, I did put them away in my room; and now they are gone and I'm perfectly sure Friker didn't take them. He would have told me. No, it wasn't the police. I think it's Cyril. I intend to get them back from him. I didn't tell Friker the reports were stolen and don't intend to. But I hate to see Kirby making a fool of you, Elizabeth. I am asking you to send him away."

But Cyril had to leave, in any case, soon—as soon as there was a boat. She wished with every fiber of

154

her will that there would be no boat and no way for him to go. At least not soon—not now. She said, "The inspector told him to stay."

Dyke brushed it aside. "He can't make him stay. He knows it. So do I."

"You don't like him, do you?" said Elizabeth slowly.

"That's not the question," said Dyke. "I'm asking you to send him away."

There was a long pause. Someone inside the house turned on the wireless again, trying for stations, and the sounds were clear and sharp, sputtering with static.

"Well?" said Dyke.

"I won't send him away, Dyke. He's got to go— soon. But I won't send him away."

"Elizabeth"—he threw away his cigarette and put both arms around her quickly. "Elizabeth," he said, "if you love me, you'll do it." His arms were warm and tight; he leaned nearer to put his face against her own. She pulled away from him though he would have held her.

"But I don't love you, Dyke," she said steadily.

"Don't love me," he began incredulously and then held her tight in his arms again, laughing a little. "Elizabeth, darling, what's wrong?"

"I'm not going to send him away, Dyke. And we— you and I—must have a clear understanding. Now."

"But darling . . ." He hesitated and then laughed again indulgently. "Now, Elizabeth, don't get all upset about this. We do understand each other. I love you and you love me. Let's not quarrel again as we did two years ago. We're going to be married as soon as—as we can. That's understood." She tried to speak but he went on quickly, "Darling, this isn't the time or place for talking about our own plans. I understand how you feel. I love you and I know that you love me. I—I still have that dear little letter you wrote to me. It is," said Dyke rather deliberately, "here in the house with me. Now then, darling—let's not talk any more of it. Except I expect you to send Kirby away. It's not much to ask of you. I don't want to remind you of anything like—well, obligation. But you did send for me, you know. And I came. Now then, darling," said Dyke softly, "let's join the others. You understand my feelings about Kirby; I leave the rest to you."

"But you must listen . . ."

"Not now, Elizabeth. Later. This isn't the time . . ."

She said wearily, "Dyke, if the helium papers are gone, you should tell the police. I don't believe that Cyril has taken them."

"You must let yourself be guided by me, Elizabeth. I love you, darling; I have your best interests at heart."

"And you ought to destroy that letter of mine, Dyke." Something chill and ugly had somehow crept out of the night. "If the inspector finds it . . ."

"Darling, don't be silly. *Me* let him get hold of a

156

letter in which you said what you said? About Uncle Bob, I mean. What an idea! Come along, darling!"

"Dyke, please give me that letter. I can't tell you how much I regret it . . ."

"All right," he said suddenly agreeable and gay again. "Tomorrow. Let me hold the door for you."

Helplessly she entered the house with him. Cyril and Charlie were in Charlie's little room under the stairs and a typewriter was going. Ruth was nowhere to be seen and Charmian was alone in the spacious, cool library, the soft black folds of the long-sleeved dinner gown she wore falling about her, as she sat in brooding silence.

Elizabeth went to the door of Charlie's little workroom, but Cyril and Charlie were bent over the heap of telegrams and cables and did not see her. She looked at the back of Cyril's blond head, at his lean square shoulders; she had believed him when he said the thing he had said, there in the garden in the soft dusk. And she still believed him.

But as she went upstairs, Dyke, watching her from the hall with a spark of something indefinable in his brown eyes, called softly up to her: "Good night, Elizabeth."

Cyril in the study must not have heard; otherwise she thought he would have come to speak to her.

She went on up the graciously curving stairway. It was not easy to pass through Robert's study but the lights were on there; the room was clean and orderly; the desk was covered. She glanced at the small wall

157

safe and thought of what Dyke had told her about the emeralds and wondered if Robert had returned them to the safe. He had said he intended to give them to someone but that probably meant exactly nothing.

Well, if Charmian wanted the emeralds she could have them. That is, if she, Elizabeth, had anything to say about it. She didn't know the safe combination, but Charlie must know it. The next day, if time permitted, they would open the safe, settle the question of the emeralds, let Charmian know where she stood.

If time permitted—that is, if the police . . .

She did not finish that thought but went quickly to her own suite.

It wasn't late but it seemed a lifetime since—almost twenty-four hours ago now—she had stood as she was then standing, in that small dressing room. And had heard revolver shots.

It would be better not to think of that, too.

Better not think either of the distance between her room and the rest of the house—with Robert's study where the night before murder had walked, intervening like a sinister barrier between her and the others.

She undressed quickly. There was a light on in her bedroom; the bed was turned down, the canopy of mosquito netting let neatly down around it, and a glass of milk stood on her bed table. She smiled a little. Marianna? But it wasn't Marianna who had brought the milk; it was Cyril, for a small note lay beside it—typed hurriedly, probably, as he and Charlie worked. It said, "Drink this, dear. Get a good sleep and don't worry. Cyril."

She began to drink it slowly, thinking in circles. But if the helium papers were gone they must tell the inspector; suddenly she saw that that disappearance might be far more important than Dyke believed it to be; it might even have an important bearing upon the murder. She didn't know how or why; but she did know that helium is scarce and valuable—and in Europe war was spreading like a plague.

She sipped the milk. Cyril and Charlie had taken all the burden of dealing with the flood of messages, and with the cabled inquiries from newspapers. Charlie tried to be helpful in spite of his fears. Charlie . . .

She put down the glass suddenly. Funny it seemed to have an odd, bitter taste. She stared at it a moment. But that was nonsense. It had only occurred to her because she was thinking of Charlie's frightened little story.

She had taken about a quarter of the glass of milk. It was, of course, absurd to imagine its taste was wrong. But she didn't want the rest of it.

She turned out the light, and in the darkness adjusted the ghostly light folds of mosquito netting around the bed. It was rather dreadful there in the dark to think that someone had murdered Robert. Someone? Well, then, who?

Better not think of that either. And then all at once, suddenly, she went to sleep.

Time must have passed, because when she began to dream that fantastic dream it was with a half-conscious sense of its being very late and the house very quiet. Yet she wasn't wholly conscious either; for she was dreaming. Dreaming horribly. Something was wrong. She was being smothered; she was suffocating, gasping, fighting, struggling for breath. It was as if a vise clamped down upon her; as if a suffocating weight pressed upon her face. She struggled and fought and was suddenly conscious.

Conscious but struggling against her own pillow which was pressed down hard across her face. Someone was there—above her in the darkness—someone strong, relentless; pressing that pillow over her face so everything was black and throbbing and there was no air anywhere and she could not move.

18

ELIZABETH began to fight for her life. Struggling, twisting, writhing away from that strong and suffocating weight. There was no air, there was no way to call for help, there was nothing but throbbing darkness and struggle.

It was horribly hard to fight—there was no air and her muscles were heavy and seemed to move with enormous difficulty. She could hear nothing but the pounding of blood in her own ears. But suddenly the pillow slipped a little and she got a breath of air and fought harder against that dreadful weight, that instantly pressed over her face again holding her down, crowding out life and breath from bursting lungs.

Again with a superb effort she twisted away from the pillow. The folds of mosquito netting choked her, the bed clothing wrapped around her and she fought that, too. Ludicrously—horribly.

And all at once something seemed to give way and

slide into the black chaos about her and she continued to struggle thrusting the suffocating pillow away from her—pushing through stubborn, soft netting, sliding out of bed—and getting a great lungful of air which stung and hurt her throat. She was panting, gasping, clutching for air and more air.

And was suddenly fully conscious—aware of the darkness and of the silence in the room. Someone must be there. But there was no sound—no motion—no faint sound of breathing. She took another great gasp of air, listened and still heard nothing.

She felt oddly sluggish as if she were weighed down with some impalpable burden. But she was now fully awake. Her head throbbed and her throat was dry and aching.

She must do something—call for help—escape before that murderous attack struck again out of the darkness around her. But she was so distant from the rest of the house that if she screamed her heart out she still could not make anyone hear.

She listened again; her heart was still so loud and fast it was the only sound she could hear. Slowly, she never knew just when, she became convinced that she was alone in the room. It was a sixth sense that convinced her of it; nothing definable. She was still too frightened and dazed to reason.

Somehow she found her way around the bed, to grope into that darkness for the bed lamp, to force her shaking hands to turn on the light. Instinct alone

162

governed her and that atavistic sense was right; no one was there.

Well, then, what next? Summon help? Have them search the house—search the grounds? The French doors opening upon the balcony were as always at night open with a strip of black night showing beyond them. Someone could have come that way—up the trellis as Dyke had come, into her room, knowing his way.

His way? Then who?

Who, and where had he gone? She sat down on the bed; she felt extraordinarily groggy and light-headed. Her knees were unsteady; her head throbbing. Funny how difficult it was to think!

But he could have escaped, too, by way of Robert's study, losing himself in the house, escaping later by way of the front door which was easily unlocked and opened from the inside.

Or not escaping.

Was it, then, someone in the house? Charmian? Ruth? Charlie? It couldn't be Dyke. It couldn't be Cyril.

But someone—one of that dreadfully short list—had murdered Robert. Hadn't they? And didn't she, in her heart, know it? Then why not another murder? Herself. It was as easy to hang for two sheep as for one. When once that dark dividing line had been crossed perhaps murder was easy.

She must get help. That was the thing to do. She couldn't just sit there shivering, waiting for him to come back. This time perhaps with a more effectual weapon than her own pillow.

Her throat ached and stung. She put out her hand toward the bell; it would ring in Marianna's room; she mustn't expose the maid to danger—answering the bell, coming alone through those dark and silent halls, through Robert's empty, dark study.

If only she could think! She pressed both hands to her throbbing temples and saw that something was gone from the bed table. Something that had been there—that had figured in her last conscious thought before she went suddenly to sleep.

The glass. That was it. There had been a glass of milk and a typed note and now both were gone.

She stared at the bed table. And got up and snatched a dressing gown from the foot of the bed and in a kind of hypnosis of stark terror did a thing that she couldn't have done if she had stopped to think. She went through the little passage, her bare feet light on the rug and into Robert's study; she did falter there at the doorway, but the opposite door into the main hall was open and a light was on in the hall so a dim lane of light led through the room. She plunged into it.

Halfway across the room it seemed to her that something moved somewhere in the blackness beyond the lane of light. At her left—in the direction of the great, blood-stained desk. There was nothing to do but go ahead and she did. She reached the hall and there was a dim light burning down at the end of it. The stair well was empty, bedroom doors closed. Which was Cyril's?

Ruth's came first, then Dyke's; Charmian had the corner room; Cyril's was around the corner and down two or three steps. Again it seemed to her that there was a sound in the study behind her; she ran lightly down the hall and around the corner and reached Cyril's door and opened it. It was, of course, in darkness.

"Cyril—Cyril . . ." Her voice was only a whisper. She closed the door behind her, fumbled against the wall for the electric light button, found and pressed it. Blinking in the light she cried again, "Cyril," and stopped, for Cyril was not there. The bed was tossed but empty; he was nowhere in the room. "Cyril," she whispered again, as if to someone who must be there, and then heard or thought she heard the soft sound of footsteps padding lightly somewhere outside the door she had just closed. But before she could have opened the door the sound stopped.

After a while she decided she couldn't have heard stealthy footsteps padding along the hall. (Stopping suddenly—at what door?) Her head was throbbing so curiously; her heart pounding. She couldn't be sure of anything. Except that now she was afraid to go back to her own room.

Cyril certainly would return. She would wait for him.

Presently she went over to a lounge chair and sat down so she could face the door. Should she turn off

165

the light or leave it burning? Should she—queer how all at once, suddenly, as soon as she sank down into that chair she was sleepy again! But that—good heavens—that was the milk! The medicine. Charlie's medicine.

And Cyril had put that glass of milk on her bed table and with a note telling her to drink it. Cyril! But she had come to him for help. She must fight that drowsiness; she must struggle out of the softly embracing armchair; she must rouse herself again and not sink into the sleep that threatened—that promised, that offered dark and quiet release.

Cyril opened the door and walked in and saw her and stopped and said, "Good God—Elizabeth!"

He wore a dark dressing gown over his pajamas and bedroom slippers with soft soles. He closed the door quickly and came toward her. "Elizabeth, what's happened? What's the matter? *Elizabeth*—" All at once he was kneeling beside her, shaking her a little, making her talk.

"Someone was there . . ."

"Don't mumble like that. Are you sick? Elizabeth . . ."

"The milk," she said drowsily. "Something in it. Somebody—pillow . . ." She had to go to sleep. There was no use fighting against it. She leaned against him, her head on his shoulders.

"Elizabeth . . ." He was shaking her again, dragging words out of her. She made a great effort and said, "Tried to smother—my own pillow . . ."

She knew that he thrust her back against the chair and rose. She opened her eyes reluctantly and had a queer glimpse of his white face and the tense set of his mouth. Then he was gone. She knew that. And all at once with no time whatever passing he was back again. He was putting things down on the table—things that clattered. He was holding a cup to her lips; he was making her drink . . .

"Hot," she gasped.

"Drink it. For God's sake, Elizabeth, drink it. Help me."

She drank. She drank more. Coffee—bitter and strong.

He was making her walk now, dragging her out of the chair. Pulling her up and down the room. Pausing to look at her small bare feet and then putting slippers of his own on them, so large that they shuffled when she walked.

"How much did you drink?"

"N—not much—quarter of a glass—Cyril, I'm so sleepy . . ."

He was relentless. As those hands had been, smothering the breath out of her, strangling—no, she mustn't think of that.

There was more hot, black coffee, so strong and bitter it was nauseous.

Once he stopped with a kind of desperate look and went to the adjoining bathroom and returned with wet, cold towels and slapped her face with them briskly. And then pushed back her soft hair with gentle hands. "Sorry," he said, "had to." And then made her walk again.

"If there was only time to get a doctor here—Elizabeth, listen. *How* much did you drink of it?"

"Only—quarter of a glass. Only—that."

It was still difficult to talk. But she was better; strength was coming back to those drugged and heavy muscles and she was perfectly aware of what was going on now—of the shining coffee pot on the table—of her shuffling slippers and long white dressing gown—so long it tripped her now and then—and of Cyril's arm holding her.

It was, however, much later before he let her stop and rest.

"I'm really all right now, Cyril. You've walked me miles up and down this room."

"Yes. Funny nobody heard us." He sat down at last opposite her.

"Now, then, if you're sure you aren't going to tumble off to sleep again, let's have the whole story."

She told him all of it; briefly, hurrying over that fantastic and horrible dream that went into more horrible reality. But when she finished, his face was a white and rigid mask with blazing eyes. He got up and came to her.

"Elizabeth," he said almost hoarsely. "Oh, my dear," and took her so tight and hard in his arms it was as if he never meant to let her go. But he did release her almost at once, and said, "And the glass is gone now?"

168

"Yes. Cyril, I'm sure of all this. I wasn't dreaming. Someone was there."

"Who? Elizabeth, *think*. Isn't there some clue? Some—voice, some motion, something?"

"Nothing that I haven't told you. I thought I heard footsteps in the hall—I don't know who it was; I don't know where the footsteps stopped."

He stood looking down at her in deep thought. She said, "Cyril, why? Why would anybody attack me like that? It was—it would have been murder."

"If you had had all the milk—if you hadn't roused— Elizabeth, I didn't put that glass of milk on your bed table; I didn't write that note."

"I know you didn't. You—you saved my life just now."

"No; I didn't save your life; probably most of whatever must have been in the glass had sunk to the bottom of it by the time you drank it. You roused enough to fight off that attack upon you—and you can thank your stars, my dear, for all the swimming and tennis playing you've done; then naturally you collapsed again. But I don't think you had taken enough of it to—to do any more than put you out for a day or so. If so, you wouldn't have come to your senses by now. But you see I couldn't be sure. It's lucky I came back just when I did. I was awake and heard some sound. I thought it was downstairs and went down to see; no one was about. No one escaped by the front door; I would have known it." He turned, thrust his hands in the pockets of his dressing gown and walked to the windows, stared out into darkness for a moment and came back. "We can find out what Charlie's doctor gave him; but the chances are it was a strong hypnotic drug; luckily you didn't get much of it. But whoever gave it to you evidently wasn't sure—as Charlie wasn't sure—exactly what was in the stuff. His only desire was to make you unconscious and—and facilitate," said Cyril, his mouth grim and hard, "smothering you with a pillow. So simple and so—so horribly easy."

Simple and easy. It was that simplicity and ease that cut down through the nightmarish quality of it. It didn't seem exactly possible that somebody in that house had set out to murder her. But a glass of milk, a pillow over her face—that was real and it had happened.

"Who?" she said stiffly. "Why?"

"Whoever murdered Robert Dakin. Naturally. And probably because he thinks Dakin told you, before he died, who killed him."

Someone knocked lightly at the door.

19

Cyril looked questioningly at Elizabeth, hesitated, and the knock came again. He went to the door.

"Oh—Dyke. Come in."

Dyke, red silk dressing gown over blue silk pajamas, hair tousled, came quickly in.

"Elizabeth! What . . ." His dark glance swerved to Cyril. "I thought I heard voices. What's happened?"

Again, barely perceptibly, Cyril hesitated. Then he said coolly, "Somebody got into Elizabeth's room, put a pillow over her face; she's all right now. Sit down."

Dyke's dark, bright eyes went swiftly around the room.

"Well, you're having a nice companionable time of it," he said. "Coffee—chat—it's three o'clock in the morning."

"Sit down," said Cyril again quite pleasantly, but with the little touch of steel below his pleasant tones that Elizabeth was learning to recognize. "Somebody also doped some milk she drank. That's the reason for the coffee. I assure you it is not merely a social occasion."

Dyke's face flushed slowly. He sat down on the end of the bed.

"I think you'd better explain just what you mean. You can't possibly mean that there was an attempt at . . ."

"Murder? That's exactly what I mean, I'm afraid."

"But, my God! Elizabeth?"

"It's perfectly true." Cyril told him the story, tersely and quickly. "Charlie had some medicine; he doesn't know what it is but says it was labeled 'poison.' The medicine has been taken from the cupboard where he kept it. And whatever was in the milk Elizabeth drank was certainly put there with a purpose. And there's no doubt something was in it; luckily she didn't drink much."

"But . . ." Dyke's flush had gone; he looked pale and queerly shocked. He stared at the rug for a moment and then said, "But who was it, Elizabeth? Don't you know who it was?"

"She doesn't know. Do you?" said Cyril directly and unexpectedly.

"I!" cried Dyke. "But I—how could I know! What induced you to say such a crazy thing as that? I didn't do it, if that's what you mean. And I . . ." he swallowed hard. "I don't know who did it." He looked at Cyril defiantly, got up and began to walk jerkily about the room. "How could I possibly know who did it? If, as you seem to think, it's whoever murdered Uncle Bob, that means—that means whoever it is, is after Elizabeth. I—I don't know anything about it. Except—except it's got to stop," said Dyke and stopped his restless pace to stare again, agitatedly, at the floor.

"We'll see that it does stop," said Cyril, watching him. "Dyke, are you sure there's nothing you know . . ."

Dyke whirled around angrily. "If I knew anything I'd tell the inspector, of course. The next thing I know you'll be accusing me of murdering Uncle Bob."

"Somebody killed him," said Cyril imperturbably.

"Somebody . . ." Dyke flushed again and stared forward, his eyes angry, his hands clenching into fists.

"Look here, Kirby, you've gone too far. I want you to get out of this house. And stop meddling in our affairs."

Cyril, looking very tall in his dark dressing gown, leaned quietly against the bedpost. "Our affairs," he quoted. "I suppose you mean . . ."

"I mean mine and Elizabeth's," cried Dyke furiously. He turned to Elizabeth. "I told you to send him away. Why didn't you do it?"

Elizabeth grasped the arms of her chair.

"You have no right to ask that, Dyke. I won't ask him to leave. I can't . . ."

Cyril interrupted. "You aren't obliged to say anything you don't want to say, you know, Elizabeth."

But Dyke must listen, must believe her, must understand.

"I've been wrong," she cried desperately. "I'm sorry. But I can't."

Dyke wasn't listening. He cried furiously, "So she's not obliged to say anything she doesn't want to say! Who said you were her protector? Who appointed you to take over our troubles? We'll get along very well without you, Kirby. The sooner you get out of the house the better. I expect you to leave this morning. And no talk about the inspector wanting you to stay. *Get out.*"

Cyril didn't look at Elizabeth; he said, "Suppose Elizabeth doesn't want me to go? It's her house, you know . . ."

"Oh, really," said Dyke. He shoved his hands in his pockets and looked at Cyril and became all at once quiet. "I see that you don't understand the situation," he said. "Elizabeth and I are to be married. As soon as possible after this thing is cleared up. Now do you see?"

Cyril looked at Elizabeth.

"Is this true, Elizabeth?"

Elizabeth stood up, her long white dressing gown falling around her, her feet unsteady in Cyril's absurdly big slippers. She had an odd glimpse of her own face in the mirror opposite—her soft hair disheveled and thrust back of her ears, her face bare and childish without powder or lipstick, her eyes startlingly dark and clear and direct. She went to Dyke who looked at her sullenly; she put her hands on his arm.

"Dyke—I asked you to come and I asked you to help me. If there was a promise made or—or implied . . ." It was as if her tongue were reluctant; she put up her head and made herself say steadily, "If I promised you anything I'll keep my promise."

He looked down at her. "But you want me to release you, don't you? Now that you've changed your mind."

"I was wrong to write you. I thought I loved you, Dyke."

"And now that I came you think something else. Why?"

She tried to answer him honestly.

"Because I was wrong. Because you—you aren't the man I remembered. It's not your fault, Dyke. It's all mine. I didn't just—just change my mind. It's because everything is—different."

Dyke's eyes flickered. Then suddenly he smiled, warmly, with all his ready and convincing charm.

"Darling," he said, "of course, I hold you to your promise. For your own good; you'll realize that one day." He clasped her hands so tightly she could not withdraw them and turned, smiling, to Cyril who had been watching quietly with no expression whatever in his face. "You'd better know the truth, Kirby," said Dyke. "Elizabeth and I have been in love with each other for a long time; since before she met and married Uncle Bob; a—a quarrel separated us. She wrote to me when she found her marriage was going on the rocks. She said she regretted our quarrel. She asked me to come and to help her. She said—a great many things. Anyway I came. And she's to marry me. Do you understand, Kirby?"

There was a pause. Then Cyril turned deliberately to Elizabeth, "This was the man, then?" he said rather gently, looking into her eyes with an expression she could not read. "The one you told me about?"

"Yes. I was wrong—I didn't know until he came. But I did write to him—I did ask him to come . . ."

Again Dyke cut into her words.

"She said a great many things in her letter. She said her marriage was a mistake; she said she would do anything to end it. I have the letter," said Dyke rather slowly. "Not, of course, that I think she really meant she would do—anything to end her marriage. Even though I know what a violent brute Uncle Bob could be, I don't think Elizabeth shot him. But I do think she had provocation. It's lucky the inspector doesn't know of that letter, for he wouldn't understand it as I do. And," said Dyke, smiling, "as you do, Kirby."

Cyril went to the table, looking down at it absently. As absently he touched the coffee pot, and poured another cup of the strong, hot liquid. "I think I understand," he said; then, very quietly. "Will you have some coffee, too, Dyke? There's a glass in the bathroom."

"But you . . ." Dyke stopped short, still smiling but his eyes suspicious.

Cyril's shoulders lifted in a kind of shrug.

"I'm not going to poison you," he said. "And Elizabeth's decisions are her own. If you and Elizabeth intend to marry, why, you intend to marry, and that's that. I won't try to stop you."

There was another pause while Cyril swirled the coffee gently in the cup, watching its circling little motion and Dyke, the bright, charming smile looking a little fixed and rigid, watched him.

If she could only think; if she could only explain, clearly, to both of them, something they must know. As if he knew what she thought, Cyril glanced at her sharply and said, "Don't talk now, Elizabeth. Go on back to bed."

"But I—I've been so wrong. Unfair to Dyke—unfair to . . ."

Cyril put down the cup and took her hand in the queerest, hardest grip. His eyes were completely impersonal. He said, "No more talk." It was like a command. He added quickly and lightly, "If tomorrow comes there'll be time for talk; if not it doesn't matter. Do have some coffee, Dyke. Frankly, my nerves rebel at dramatics at three o'clock in the morning."

Dyke ignored the coffee. But he said, all charm and friendliness with only his eyes watchful, "So you see, Kirby, why I have every right to ask you to leave. Are you going?"

Cyril looked meditatively at the cup on the table.

"Do you want me to go, Elizabeth? Now, I mean?"

"No."

"Then I'm afraid," said Cyril, taking up the cup of coffee again, "—unless there's a boat to England sooner than I think there will be—you'll have to throw me out, old chap. Sorry and all that. Now suppose we have a quiet smoke and then go back to bed. It isn't much good getting out the police to search the place; whoever it was that attempted to smother Elizabeth has had plenty of time to get away. Have a cigarette?"

"No, thank you," said Dyke after a moment. He yawned, and smiled. "I think you'll regret your decision, Kirby. However, I'm going to spend the rest of the night in Uncle Bob's study. Come along, Elizabeth, darling, I'll go with you."

"A good idea," said Cyril. "Oh, by the way, Elizabeth; the thing I told you last night—in the garden—remember?"

"Yes . . ." She moved a step toward him. He glanced at her quickly. Her short hair was disheveled; two soft curls clung to her temples like a child's. Her face was lifted to him; her direct gray eyes dark with trouble, her mouth, which could smile so gaily and courageously, had now a sad, troubled line. He looked away. And said brusquely, "Forget it. Good night, Elizabeth."

"But—Cyril . . ." She hesitated, trying to read his averted face.

178

"Sorry," he said. "But that's what I mean. Run along. You'll take your death of cold."

She turned away, bewildered. At the door she glanced back expecting some further word or look— she didn't know what. But he was drinking coffee meditatively, very tall in his dark blue flannel dressing gown; his light hair ruffled, his face a little tired and thoughtful. He didn't turn or speak and Dyke said, "Come on! Hurry up, Elizabeth."

She went along the hall with him. He searched the whole wing quickly, said that no one was there now; that he would be on the sofa in the study and she must call out if she was frightened. He hesitated then.

"Elizabeth, who was it?"

"I don't know, Dyke."

"But you must know. Wasn't there anything—any clue . . ."

"None. Dyke, I was wrong. About everything. But will you . . ."

"Will I release you? No, my dear. Trust me, Elizabeth; I love you, darling. I only want what is best for you." His brown eyes were smiling. And evasive. He said again, "Call out if you hear anything . . ."

And went away.

The large, feather-filled pillow lay on the floor; she took it up soberly. She left the light burning on the bed table. Once, a long time after it seemed to her, there was some slight sound on the balcony outside her room; she sat up and listened, but it was not repeated and she decided at last it was only a light breeze in the vines that overhung the balustrade.

She must make Dyke understand. She couldn't make that tragic mistake another time.

Gray dawn began to touch the hilltops behind the villa. The sea turned gray, too, and blended with a fog that crept in heavily and lay like a shroud upon the hills, and masked the ravines and valleys in sluggish gray veils. The sea was quiet—ominously quiet under that gray cloud. The rainy season was past and the hurricane season was past so there was no real threat in that darkness and fog; it only lay there, sullen and heavy, blotting out the sun and sea, laying gray wraiths in the garden and through the ravine that lay, a precipitous waste of tangled mangrove and palmetto, beyond the garden. The great banyan tree, a multiple tree, spreading hugely at the garden steps, was clothed in fog and stillness, like an eerie company of sentinels.

Cyril watched it emerge indistinctly from the night. When it was full morning, but still gray and foggy, Cyril got down from the balcony, groping his way cautiously among the thick vines for the sturdy, ladder-like trellis below them. He was cold and cramped from his long vigil. He made his way quietly along the wet terrace and in at the front door which he had left unlocked and up to his own room. No one saw him.

He took a hot shower and then a cold one and then sat for a long time smoking and thinking.

Seven o'clock came and eight, and by mid-morning

the fog had not lifted but lay in wreaths in the great banyan tree and hung still in a dense gray veil over the ravine, and crept upon the wet terrace and pressed in at the windows.

Two things occurred that morning.

An empty glass, rinsed thoroughly, was found on the top steps of the stairway. It was found by the maid, Helene, who did the chamber work and reported to Flemming who reported it to Charlie in Cyril's hearing.

Charlie said, "Glass? Well, what about it?"

"It only seemed—odd, sir," said Flemming. "There were no extra glasses in any of the bedrooms, Helene says. And no glasses missing. This came from the kitchen."

"Bring it to me," said Cyril.

But it was rinsed and dry; no vestige of milk or anything else clung to its glittering sides.

"I suppose," said Cyril, "that was as good a place to leave it as any."

"Leave it? What on earth do you mean?" demanded Charlie.

"Nothing," said Cyril. "Let's go on with these letters."

He told Elizabeth about it later that day. After her momentous interview with Inspector Friker.

For that was the second thing that happened that morning. Friker came about eleven and asked to see her at once.

Marianna came to tell her; she dressed quickly.

Her hand went out from habit toward a light dress

—tailored and simple—when she saw that Marianna had put out black. A thin black silk, barely touched with white at the throat.

She looked at it, struck with a realization that it was as if, in death, the past two years of Robert Dakin's life didn't count. It was as if Charmian was his widow. Or, even, Ruth. It was her duty to observe every form and every motion of respect due him. Sometime perhaps she would remember only and with pity the last thing he had said to her. But now it would be a blatant, even an impertinent, hypocrisy for her, Elizabeth, to mourn the end of two wretched years. Even to pretend to mourn it. She wore what normally she would have worn; a plain gray cotton dress, with a jacket and a cherry-colored belt; she glanced at herself in the mirror as she started downstairs and was so struck with the pallor and weariness of her face that she went back to touch her lips slightly with a cherry-colored lipstick; to arrange her smooth, red-gold hair more carefully; to try to hide the faint blue marks under her eyes with powder.

But the inspector was waiting and she must hurry. The house was quiet and, that morning, dark. He was in the library, pacing up and down. When she entered he turned and said abruptly. "Madam, I came to tell you that unless you can give us more evidence to the contrary than you have so far given us I shall be forced to arrest you for the murder of your husband. You do realize that—don't you?"

20

THERE WAS a little pause. The heavy, brooding silence in the house settled down and around them like a fog—almost as palpable, certainly as penetrating, creeping into every corner and every shadow of the spacious, dreary room. Hiding back of the window curtains; gathering itself together behind the chair in the corner, waiting.

Friker waited, too. His fine, vivid face was clear and sharp; his look as hard and as brilliant as she remembered it. The stain of red in his cheeks and his lips seemed, that gray morning, a little dulled, and he smoked wearily and a little nervously, watching her above the gray smoke which—as if combating that impalpable thing that lay all over the house—clung together, too, in small clouds that drifted slowly and sluggishly upward. But there was in his direct manner, in his look, in the thing he said, again an irrefutable quality of truth-telling which, as always with truth, had power.

She came forward slowly and he waited until she

sat down in one of the great armchairs which Robert, some time or other, had bought from a forgotten greathouse and which had made the voyage to Jamaica on a sailing ship—taking seven weeks for the journey from England. Her feet dangled above the floor, but she clasped the heavy carved arms as if they were a bulwark. The inspector sat, then, as before, on the corner of the long table.

"I don't need to repeat myself," he said with a little impatience. "I'm sure you understand me."

"Yes. Yes, I understood. I'm only trying to think of further evidence. That's what you expect of me, isn't it? To save myself?"

"Naturally."

"Well, then. There was an attack upon me last night."

"Really?" he said politely and skeptically.

She subdued a rising spark of anger which she couldn't afford.

"It's quite true," she said soberly. "I have no proof. But it happened."

"Tell me."

She did so, quickly, under his sharp questions.

"And you think this glass of milk—which so conveniently disappeared—had in it the so-called medicine Mr. Hawes claims to have lost?"

"Yes, I do. Otherwise . . ."

"Otherwise you would not have felt as you did? Who was it that tried to smother you with the pillow?"

184

"I don't know. There was nothing—no clue at all . . ."

"Are you quite sure there was someone?"

"I am sure," she said steadily.

"And the typewritten note, signed by Mr. Kirby, urging you to drink the milk—what about that?"

She stared at him. "But I didn't tell you . . ."

"No, no. You preferred to shield your friend, Mr. Kirby. Perhaps I'd better tell you that he reached me with this—story early this morning. He told me about the note . . ."

"But he didn't write it. Cyril . . ."

"Yes, yes; so he told me. Go on, please. What of this gun Charlie Hawes says is missing also?"

"He—I think he may be mistaken." But was Charlie mistaken? She was sure, now, that he had been right about the medicine. Then the gun—and that silent, brooding house, waiting in the fog . . .

"Dear me," said the inspector. "A murderous attack in the night. A package of painkiller from the dispensary of an English doctor; a gun—from God knows where. Have you any more evidence to offer, Madam?"

Again she had to ignore the skepticism in his tone. "Yes, there's something else." They must be told about the helium reports; Dyke was wrong to try to keep the knowledge from them. She told him that, too.

It seemed to her that this time there was more credulity in his questions. He said, "And you think the loss of the helium reports might have some bearing upon the murder?"

"Yes, I do. I don't know how or why. But I do know that anything concerning helium is valuable. Particularly since the war."

"As information, do you mean? Or as a possession?" he asked, watching her.

"It would have to be as information," she said slowly. "At least there is no private production of helium."

"Oh, you do know that. Well, we'll add to our list of painkiller and gun the reports of the possibility for producing helium from oil lands in Texas." If anyone so coldly incisive could be said to have a softer quality, then he would be said to have been slightly indulgent at that moment.

"I'm telling you the truth."

"Do go on, Madam. Is there anything else?"

She hesitated. "You understand, Mr. Friker, that naturally I have thought of almost nothing but this. I've tried to remember everything, no matter how small, that could possibly have anything to do with it."

"Naturally. Have you come to any conclusions?"

"No. If by that you mean the—the identity of the murderer."

"What else, Madam! But you were about to tell me . . ."

"Yes. You see, one of the small things yet—yet puzzling—is this. When we found my husband, we found on the desk, below the arm that was—was doubled under him as he fell across the desk, something I had never seen before."

He was interested; there was an icy little flame, like the hard reflection of light in the facet of a diamond, in his gaze. "Well . . ."

"Monkeys," said Elizabeth.

"Monkeys!" There was a very slight change in his face. "Did you say . . ."

"A little carved, wooden piece." She explained it.

"Oh, yes, I understand. I've seen them. Describe this particular little figure, please, Madam."

"It was small, wooden; it looked—well, shabby. The sharp edges were worn. It looked as if—as if it had been carried in a pocket perhaps a long time."

There was a little pause. Then Friker said, "Madam is a keen observer. Who was present in the room when you observed these—monkeys?"

"Everyone. Charlie Hawes, Ruth, Dyke, Cyril."

"They can authenticate your story, then?"

"Certainly," she said coldly.

"Madam, the monkeys were not there when I arrived. I assure you of that. So you see one of those people you have named must have taken the monkeys. And thus some one of them recognized the little figures; and that recognition induced that person to remove them. Why?"

He looked at her as if he expected an answer. She said, "I suppose because of some significance . . ."

"A clue leading to the murderer. A mistake, perhaps? Something forgotten? But something recognized by your husband, too, Madam. And of a significance there as well."

He believed her; that was something.

"A clue?"

There was again that thin veil of impatience about him.

"But naturally, Madam. A thing that linked your husband with the murderer, perhaps. A thing that might have been recognized by other people and its true significance discovered. A mistake . . ."

"Mistake?"

His bright hard gaze had been remote and speculative. Now it sharpened again and focused upon her. "Naturally," he said again. "If murderers made no mistakes we would have a much more difficult time, we police. But murderers are human; and if they were not inclined toward faulty thinking, slightly off balance, they would not commit murders. It gives the police a leg up. And God knows we need it sometimes." He checked his little excursion into humanity. "What was said of those monkeys, Madam? Did anyone recognize them?"

She thought back. "N-no," she said slowly. "That is, no one said he recognized them. Ruth said—I think she said that she was sure she had seen them before; it seemed to me she was trying to remember where. I think—yes, I'm sure she felt a kind of familiarity about them. Yet she didn't seem to think they were some keepsake of my—of Robert's. Dyke thought they were a keepsake; he suggested that. Charlie said nothing. I had never seen them before and think I said so. Cyril, of course, knew nothing about them."

"But Miss Reddington—Ruth—had some faint memory that concerned the monkeys?"

"Yes. Yes, I think she had. She looked a little startled, as if trying to recall something almost forgotten." She glanced at the inspector. And thus saw the door close. Over his shoulder, off in the shadow at the end of the room. It was the faintest motion, half-seen, wholly silent. She sprang to her feet. "The door!" She pointed and Friker whirled and without pausing to question her, slid across the room and opened the door and vanished into the hall. There were at the most three or four seconds' time between her startled realization that the door had closed—as if it had been open the barest inch or two—and the inspector's emergence into the hall. Who had been there? Who had listened? Who had closed it so stealthily? As stealthily as someone had taken himself away, losing himself in the midnight darkness of the house, the night before.

The shadows of the room crept closer; she went to the table and turned on a light there. It shone on her hand and on the slender wedding ring almost concealed by the enormous star sapphire Robert had given her at the time of their marriage. The star in it winked and shone; the weight of it had always been heavy on her hand.

How quiet the house was! How quiet that room.

189

She whirled around and almost cried out when Friker suddenly opened the door and came back into the room. This time he closed the door behind him hard and went to stand before the bookshelves opposite so the wide, blank panels of the door were directly within his range of vision.

"No one in the hall," he said. "Charlie Hawes and Cyril Kirby were in the little workroom under the stairs and said they had not left the room or seen anyone. No one is in the drawing room. No one in the hall leading to the morning room, at the north end of the house. No one there. That leaves the stairway . . ." He broke off abruptly and added, "You are perfectly sure there was someone at the door?"

"I saw it close. It was only the smallest motion but —but I did see it."

It was never possible to tell how much he believed, how much he disbelieved—how much he reserved for his own rigid rules of testing.

He said, "I will inquire about the monkeys, Madam. And the gun. I asked Mr. Hawes to come in here, now. He was on the telephone; it may be a moment or two. In the meantime—I told you in the beginning it was a good plan for you to stick to the truth. Very well; I shall follow my own precepts."

It seemed to her that he took almost an arrogant satisfaction in putting cards on the table. Yet perhaps he displayed only those cards he chose to display.

"I think you'd better know that so far we have been unable to trace the ownership of the gun that killed your husband. For it was the gun that we found behind the bookshelf in your bedroom, Madam, that killed him. My own knowledge of ballistics was sufficient to prove that. As long as we cannot trace the ownership of the gun, as long as our case against Madam has any loopholes for a lawyer to shoot at, I refuse to make an arrest. It is never my desire to—lose a case," he said as unemotionally as if he meant a case of bananas. "Also it is not my desire to call in outside help. Our staff is small in comparison to that of a big city, but up to now sufficient. In the end, I must remind you, our own Magistrate's Court will try the case. It has not been long since the murder; sometimes it takes months to sew the whole thing together. I do not want anything but the truth; so in your own defense, Madam, don't permit yourself to make any statement that can't be proved. But there is something I want you to tell me. Exactly what were Miss Reddington's relations with yourself and with your husband?"

"Ruth . . ."

"Certainly. I know she had worked for your husband for many years; I know that her position in your husband's business was far more important and executive than that of even a highly efficient and confidential secretary; I know her salary to the penny and it was extraordinarily generous. I know of their long association. Well, then?"

"She—she was a very good friend," said Elizabeth slowly. "Naturally . . ."

"A good friend of yours," said the inspector, "or your husband's?"

"She didn't know me."

"Don't lie, Madam. She hates you. I saw that—instantly. It is absurdly evident. Why?"

"She never saw me before she came here. That was only the day before the murder."

The inspector laughed shortly. "You need not lie to protect another woman; Miss Reddington is anything but defenseless; she does not need lies from you. Listen to me, Madam. I suggest that she has been in love with your husband for many years. I suggest that she was instrumental in bringing about your husband's divorce from his first wife. Please don't interrupt. The first Mrs. Dakin admitted as much. She said in so many words that it was Ruth who influenced Robert Dakin to agree to a divorce, to arrange evidence which would secure a divorce—collusion, in other words—and that it was Ruth who influenced him to give the first Mrs. Dakin the extremely large alimony he did give her. I suggest that Ruth's motive was marriage—marriage to the man she loved perhaps for a very long time, Major Robert Dakin. And then—then he married you. I suggest that, and this is a mere possibility, and only if I am unable to prove the better and stronger case I have," he made a kind of bow as if in apology, "against Madam herself, I suggest that revenge has been the motive for many a murder. And that Ruth Reddington had that motive."

"Not Ruth . . ."

"Again—only as an alternative, remember—there are certain points which lead to Ruth Reddington. One is the fact that her trip from Kingston to Montego Bay did not occur exactly as she told it. Another is that she has many dependents and is very likely to have been remembered in Major Dakin's will; this point we shall prove today, when we, with Madam's permission, take a look at this will. Mr. Hawes says it is in the house. Another point, which Miss Reddington shares with yourself, Madam, is that she has no alibi for the time when the murder was committed. And the last one is that there are marks below Miss Reddington's bedroom windows showing where a ladder rested. Clear marks in the turf which were there the morning after the crime, which were photographed and of which a mold was taken. Yesterday the ladder itself was found—hidden under some heavy shrubs in the ravine. The ends of the ladder fit our molds exactly. The windows of the study are directly above the terrace where ladder marks would not show. Now then, Madam, you see what your hope for freedom is. Can you add anything to the evidence we already have against Ruth Reddington?"

But that was unfair. That was ugly and hideous, yet words Ruth had spoken returned to her. And words Cyril had said, "relentless" he had called Ruth. "A dangerous enemy."

Charlie Hawes opened the door and came in. She saw at a glance that he had turned sulky and stubborn.

His hands were unsteady; he gripped the back of a chair as if to hide that unsteadiness.

"I wanted to ask you," said the inspector, "about the medicine and the gun which you told Mrs. Dakin and Mr. Kirby about. I realize that anyone in the house had access to the medicine. But was there ever a second key to the filing cabinet from which the gun was taken? And was the gun loaded?"

"Medicine?" said Charlie after a long moment. "Gun? I don't know what you're talking about."

21

THE ANNOYING thing was, that in spite of everything, he stuck to his denial. Even when Friker sent for Cyril and both Cyril and Elizabeth tried to reason with him, Charlie still shook his head stubbornly, avoided their eyes and said he didn't know anything about a gun. Or about a package of medicine. And he'd thank them to let him get back to his work.

"Listen, you little—" Cyril, white and angry, grasped Charlie's thin arm. "You told me and you told Mrs. Dakin about it—there in the garden, last night before dinner. If you don't tell the truth now I'll . . ."

"No violence, please, Mr. Kirby," said the inspector. "We'll search the house for the medicine and for the gun, in any case. Perhaps later Mr. Hawes will—remember it." His bright, hard look dismissed Charlie. He said, "There's something else. What about this small image of monkeys that was on Major Dakin's desk when he was found dead? Did you see that, Mr. Kirby?"

"Yes. Yes, certainly. Why?"

"Do you know who took it away?"

"I—I didn't know anyone took it away," said Cyril. A thoughtful look came in his face. "See here," he said, "I thought nothing at all about that. Is there anything . . ."

"Did you see the monkeys, Mr. Hawes?" inquired the inspector. Charlie thought about it a moment, and then said sulkily that, yes, he thought he had.

"Had you ever seen them before?"

No, he was certain he had not. He still avoided Elizabeth's eyes and still looked frightened and stubborn.

"Who took them away?"

Charlie didn't know. He had never thought about it again. Anyway, they were not important.

The inspector took a long breath. "Monkeys, missing papers, painkiller, a gun," he said softly. "That's all."

"Do you mean . . ." began Cyril.

"I said that's all," snapped Friker. "You may go. All of you. But, Mrs. Dakin, will you please think over what I've told you. And if you can discover any evidence bearing upon the suggestion I have just made, I need not repeat that it is decidedly to your interest to tell me."

He went away without another word, so swiftly, in fact, that Charlie looked startled and then ducked like a rabbit for the door in order to precede him and avoid being left in the library with Cyril and Elizabeth.

But you couldn't reason with Charlie, you couldn't do anything with him when he turned sulky.

"Why did he deny it?"

"Scared," said Cyril. "Heard something of the affair last night; probably afraid the inspector will think his story of losing the medicine was a lie; that Friker will think Charlie tried to—kill you—last night. There's no accounting for Charlie's peculiar mental twists. All that is certain is that he's scared for his life. Elizabeth, what had Friker to say? Anything in particular?" He looked anxious in spite of the careful casualness of his tone.

"He didn't arrest me." She sat down and leaned her head back against the chair. She felt queerly bound; as if a net had secretly spread itself all around her and there was now no way to escape its entangling ropes. She clasped her hands together to steady them, and looked up at Cyril.

He was watching her, smiling a little, looking in the cool, sand-colored slacks and lounge coat he wore —like white linen, almost a uniform in the tropics— exactly as he always looked, quite matter-of-fact, pleasant, a little casual, as if none of the horror and nightmare could touch him. Only his eyes were too intent. And he said nothing at all of Dyke; nothing at all of the thing he had told her, there in the garden, and then told her to forget.

"Well, then . . ." he said.

Well, then—there was Ruth! "It seems there's an alternative."

197

Cyril frowned; one hand went up to tug a little at his short, sandy moustache. "I should say there were at least five alternatives."

"There's one choice."

"Ruth?"

"How did you know?"

"Because it's my choice, too."

"Your choice?" She sat up quickly. *"Ruth?"*

"What's the motive he gives her? Revenge, I suppose. Because Dakin married you?"

She nodded.

"If that's so," said Cyril still quietly, "I'm sure it must have occurred to you that she . . ." He broke off abruptly. "Listen, Elizabeth. I didn't say this last night but I must say it now. There was an attack upon you last night that ought not to have failed. I mean it was sheer chance that it did fail; you didn't drink all the milk; you became conscious; you were able to fight back. But that was chance . . ." he hesitated.

"What are you trying to tell me?"

"I'm trying to say that—that the next time chance might not operate. Do you see? If you were dangerous to somebody last night, you are still dangerous today. Whoever did it—Ruth, or whoever it was—did it because they think you know something incriminating."

"But I don't . . ."

"You mean you think you don't. I don't know what it is; I've gone over and over everything you've told me and I can't find the clue. At least"—he stopped there thoughtfully and then went on—"it's those few minutes you were alone with him, I think; whoever did it must believe that Dakin told you who shot him. And that—for some reason—you haven't yet told the inspector. Since Friker has made no arrests there's just a chance that, today, whoever murdered him will begin to believe that you've told the truth, after all, about those moments and that you really don't know who did it. There's just a chance that if the murderer is gradually convinced of that, you won't be in danger. But I'm only guessing about all of it. So the only safe course—if it is safe—is not to give the murderer another chance. That is, try to stay within call of other people. Eat only what the others—oh, well, that's preposterous I suppose. Poison's not a very easy weapon, and the supply of Charlie's painkiller must have been used up. The empty glass was found, you know," he said, and told her about it quickly. "The trouble is there's nothing in the glass to prove our story; and the note is gone. But the thing I'm trying to tell you, Elizabeth, is that there are easier, quicker, simpler weapons even than—than were used last night. Although that had a kind of fiendish simplicity. But don't you see, Elizabeth, someone here—in this house—murdered Robert Dakin and tried to murder you. Charmian, Ruth, Dyke—let me finish—Dyke's a suspect too; so is Charlie. So am I. Except I didn't do it. But that's what everyone says. I didn't mean to frighten you; sorry."

"I—I knew all that."

"Sorry I let myself go on at such length," he said.

"Well, . . ." He went to the table, took a cigarette from the box, held it unlighted in his hand and said, "I went to see Leech early this morning. He's still unconscious but much better. Friker has been wanting to question Leech, you know; he will as soon as he is conscious. Is there anything Leech knows, Elizabeth, that—that might be damaging to you?"

"Only what the inspector already knows," she said.

"You're sure of that?"

"Reasonably sure."

He was frowning as thoughtfully at the little white cylinder in his fingers as if he had never seen a cigarette before.

"It struck me," he said, "that there was a lot of solicitude about Leech; I mean on the part of the others. Charmian—Dyke—Ruth—all of them inquired about him. Has anyone said anything to you?"

"About Leech? Why—why, yes. Ruth. But it was only an inquiry. It didn't strike me as anything particularly urgent on her part."

"Tell me what they have against Ruth," said Cyril.

She told him briefly. When she finished he said that he, too, had seen the marks of the ladder and marks of the mold of it the police had taken. "They used some kind of plastic material with an agar base, I imagine." He glanced at the door. "I think our Mr. Friker is returning."

He was. And he had a suggestion. It was made so politely and so briefly that it didn't sound like the order that it was.

200

Mr. Hawes had informed him that a copy of Major Dakin's will was kept in the wall safe, upstairs in the study. And Mr. Hawes, who knew the combination, would open the safe. Therefore the inspector suggested that they open the will and read it. "If," said the inspector, looking at Elizabeth, "none of the members of the family object. It is not customary to take things into your own hands like this; and if you wish to wait until you can procure your own lawyer from the States, or another lawyer, I will be perfectly willing for you to do so. On the other hand, opening and reading the will right now might possibly expedite our inquiry. I don't want to insist, however. Do you agree to it, Mrs. Dakin?"

"Oh, yes," said Elizabeth.

"Look here, Friker," said Cyril. "Hawes was lying just now, you know. I'm convinced that he meant what he told us last night; that is, that a gun is missing. I wish—I wish you'd find it."

Friker's black, knife-thin eyebrows went up. "The house is being searched."

"But a gun . . ." said Cyril slowly. "A gun is so— so quick. And easy."

There was a little pause while the two men looked at each other. It struck Elizabeth briefly that there was some like quality about them, something hard and tempered.

Charlie was waiting for them in the study and opened the safe. His hands were nervous; he found difficulty twirling the two little dials. Ruth was there, perfectly controlled, neat and smart in her hand-knitted, beautifully fitting blue suit and white blouse. The light was on and gleamed in a blue highlight on her smooth, short black hair and the black widow's peak on her white forehead. She was perfectly silent; only her dark eyes were watchful and observant.

Charmian was beside her; she had a right to be there. She spoke quietly to Elizabeth when she entered the room; she was dressed carefully and effectively as always; her pale green gown, with its soft white collar and white cuffs, clung to her extraordinarily slender figure; her thin face with its intellectual forehead and wide, emotional, somewhat petulant mouth was in repose. But it was a repose that was maintained, Elizabeth thought, only because Charmian had chosen that particular pose. For she was knitting rapidly, her long fingers flashing quickly in and out, as if her taut nerves found relief in her fingers' activities and her eyes glittered and shone under those languid, weary eyelids; they were impatient; they were secretive. And they held deep in their green depths again that spark of unfriendliness.

Dyke came in late, spoke to no one, and stood leaning on the back of Ruth's chair, watching Charlie.

The inspector himself took the folded paper from the envelope Charlie Hawes handed him. He glanced at it swiftly.

Charmian's jeweled, thin hands flashed in her knitting. Ruth's dark eyes lifted to fix somberly upon the inspector. Dyke listened eagerly; yet Dyke knew the main provisions of the will; he had known for years that he was the heir.

Friker said, "Shall I read this word for word . . ."

"Tell us what it is," said Dyke. "We needn't hear all the legal phrases."

"Very well," said Friker. "It's quite simple. There are a few provisions, moderate sums for servants. This house and the house in England go to Elizabeth Dakin, until (if) she remarries. Then they revert to the estate." He paused, looking at the will uncertainly as if about to reread it. Dyke was frowning. "And the estate—the business—the money? What about that?"

"All the business property, all his estate in fact, real and personal, goes to Miss Ruth Reddington. With the exception of a trust fund of fifty thousand dollars for Dyke Sanderson." The inspector said it very slowly and deliberately.

After a moment Ruth rose, grasping the arms of her chair so tightly that she seemed to be thrusting her slender body upward. "To me?" she said stiffly.

"That's wrong! There's a mistake! You're not reading it correctly. Give it to me . . ." Dyke crossed the room at a leap and seized the will.

Friker relinquished it readily.

"It is in paragraph three," he said. "There . . ." he pointed.

"But this—I can't believe this," cried Dyke harshly. He stared at the inspector, stared at Ruth, thrust back his dark hair and read it again. He was curiously gray under his tan. Ruth said, "Are you sure, Inspector? Isn't there a mistake?"

"There's no mistake," said the inspector. "You can read it yourself."

Charmian rose with a little soft rustle of silk. "I didn't expect any provision made for me. I—take it there is none."

"None, Madam."

"And the—emeralds?" said Charmian calmly, holding her pose of disinterest as deftly as any actress.

"The emeralds go to the second Mrs. Dakin. Mr. Hawes tells me there is a copy of the will with Major Dakin's lawyer in America. There is no doubt that it is genuine. Miss Reddington . . ."

Ruth did not seem to hear him. She was standing perfectly still, her face white, her lips tight together.

"Miss Reddington," said Friker again, sharply.

Her blank gaze shifted to him.

He said, "Miss Reddington, after Robert Dakin was murdered a small wooden figure was found on this desk, below his hand. It was a wooden figure, a carving of three small monkeys. Had you ever seen it before? Do you know where? Do you remember it?"

"Why—why, yes," said Ruth, her eyes and face still curiously blank. Then all at once, so palpably that they could see it, she seemed to come alive. Her face became mobile; her hands went to her throat, to her mouth. She said loudly and violently, "That is, no! No! I have never seen it before. Never."

22

IT SEEMED to Elizabeth that it was exactly at that instant that all pretense vanished.

It was as if the mention of the monkeys stripped all polite veils from the faces of those around her; broke down guards, thrust aside all the thin barriers they had erected, each for his own protection.

This was murder; Robert Dakin had died, painfully, lying across the desk; and a small, carved piece of wood had something to do with that murder. It was as clear and plain as if the knowledge had taken body to itself, and tangibility, and had stood before them, another presence in the room.

All at once Ruth was completely composed again. Charmian sat down with a soft little rustle of silk. Dyke looked up from the will and folded the paper with a crisp rattle. Charlie, hovering beside the safe, said, "I'll put that back in the safe, Sanderson. After everyone has seen it."

And the inspector said, "Do you know anything about the monkeys, Sanderson?"

Dyke wrenched his gaze from the will.

"What? Oh, the monkeys. Yes, I saw them. But I don't know anything about them or what happened to them."

"By the way, Sanderson, when you and Miss Reddington arrived at Montego Bay the night before the murder . . ." The inspector checked himself and slid his real inquiry in gently and adroitly, "You did arrive together?"

"Yes, of course." It was Dyke who replied. Ruth said nothing.

"And in the same car—driving from Kingston to Montego Bay?"

There was a quality of hesitation in the little silence before Dyke spoke. "Oh," he said. "I didn't understand you. We arrived in Kingston together; we came on the same plane from Miami. That's what I meant when you asked me if we had come here together and I said we had."

"Did you have that impression from my inquiry, too, Miss Reddington?" said Friker.

She seemed to draw herself from some distant, absorbing thought. "Yes—yes, I think so."

"But you two actually did not travel together from Kingston?"

Again there was a tinge of hesitation in the silence. Ruth looked at the inspector with a clouded, absent expression in her fine dark eyes. And Dyke replied,

"Well, no—as you seem to know. As a matter of fact we crossed the island in different cars. We arrived at Montego Bay at about the same time; we met in the hotel and dined together. And later hired a car and a driver who brought us up here."

"Was that by prearrangement?"

Dyke frowned. "No. I thought Ruth had come directly to the villa—here, I mean—and didn't expect to meet her in the hotel. But I was hungry and stopped there and she was there, too, in the lounge waiting for dinner to be served. Naturally we ate together and then came on out here."

"Why didn't you take the same car from Kingston to Montego Bay? It's over a hundred-mile drive—a hundred and eighteen to be exact."

Dyke shrugged. "We'd arrived the day before by plane from Miami. Naturally we stayed in Kingston that night intending to come on to Montego Bay by car the next day; as we did. But not together, because Ruth wanted to shop a bit in Kingston. I thought I would come on ahead. But I didn't; I overslept and got a latish start; actually she was ahead of me on the road, but I didn't know that, and, anyway, it didn't matter."

"What time exactly did you arrive in Montego Bay, Mr. Sanderson?"

"What time?" Dyke's eyes narrowed. "Why—I don't know. Not long before dinner."

"And you, Miss Reddington?"

Ruth's eyes were intent now but, which was odd,

puzzled. "Why—about the same time as Dyke, I imagine; I hadn't been at the hotel long when he came in."

Friker sighed gently.

"You arrived at the hotel in Montego Bay at three in the afternoon, Miss Reddington; you dismissed the car that you came in. Then you walked along the street toward the town. You returned about an hour and a half later and sat in the hotel lounge until dinner time, when Mr. Sanderson arrived. And you, Mr. Sanderson, arrived in Montego Bay just after four, dismissed your car and likewise disappeared for about two hours. Exactly where did you go and what did you do?"

Again there was a look of perplexity and faint surprise on Ruth's face; oddly, it was duplicated for an instant in Dyke's face. Then he said, "I went for a walk; I used to come here with Uncle Bob and I knew the town and simply wanted to prowl around and see it again. That's all."

"And you, Miss Reddington?"

Ruth hesitated, and then said slowly, "Well, as a matter of fact that's what I did. There was no hurry about our coming to the house here; we weren't expected for dinner—indeed, Bob and Elizabeth were going out to dinner, although, of course, I didn't know that. There was really no ulterior motive in our coming so far to see Bob and then lingering a little for dinner in Montego Bay before coming out here. It just—happened that way."

"Eventually I'll find out the truth," said Friker. "Why not tell me now?"

Impatience flashed in Dyke's face. "We have told you the truth! What on earth could either of us do in Montego Bay that has any bearing on Uncle Bob's murder! Or his"—his face darkened as he glanced again at the will in his hand and he cried—"or his will. How dared he do this to me! How dared . . ." He thrust the will at Charlie and strode quickly out of the room. He didn't look at Elizabeth; he didn't look at anybody.

Ruth said quickly, "Dyke—wait—I didn't know it was to be this way." He did not return and Charlie, rummaging in the safe, said suddenly, "Oh, I say! The emeralds aren't here!" He turned with a flat leather jewel case in his hand. It was open, the white velvet lining obviously empty. He held it out toward the inspector. His small mouth quivered, his eyes darted from one to another of them. He said, "I didn't take them. I didn't open the safe. I . . ."

"Oh, be still, Charlie," said Ruth almost impatiently. "I have the emeralds. He gave them to me. They belong to you now, Elizabeth. I'll get them." She hesitated; there was still a look of deep perplexity on her face as she turned and walked out of the room. But her footsteps along the hall did not stop at her own room; Elizabeth, listening, was sure of that and almost equally sure that she went to Dyke's room.

And Charmian said, with a faint, mocking smile on her lips, and that spark of enmity in her eyes, that that was settled. "Congratulations, Elizabeth," she said. "The emeralds are a small fortune, you know, in themselves. I chose each stone and I know."

Emeralds? But she didn't want them; she couldn't take them. She said quickly, "The emeralds are yours, Charmian, if you want them."

Charmian stared at her and sat forward so abruptly that her knitting bag dropped, spilling its contents completely. The inspector, nearest her, politely retrieved knitting, needles, balls of yarn, handkerchief, powder compact. Charmian said, staring at Elizabeth, "Do you mean . . ."

"I don't want them. It's not generosity. You needn't hesitate about taking them. I—I hate them."

"Oh," said Charmian. "Oh, I—very well. Thank you, Elizabeth," she added perfunctorily.

Charlie closed the case with a snap and returned it to the safe. The closing jar of the safe door seemed to end the interview. Charlie walked to the door, said nervously to Elizabeth, "The will is all in order. When your lawyers are ready to see it . . ." He stopped indecisively, glanced at Charmian and back at Elizabeth and said, "The emeralds . . ." clicked his tongue, shook his head and went away.

The inspector followed him.

Charmian said coolly, "Charlie's easily upset. But then he never was a mine of courage; it's funny he stayed with Robert so long. What's all this about monkeys? What monkeys?"

Cyril, who had been watching the whole scene, explained.

"But—but who took them away, then?" asked Charmian. "Someone must have done it. And why?"

Cyril shrugged. "I don't know. I didn't."

"But naturally—I mean both Ruth and Dyke seemed . . ." Charmian stopped. After a moment's thought she rose. "Thank you for the emeralds, Elizabeth," she said calmly and walked out of the room, her green gown and her big tapestry knitting bag fading into the shadows of the hall.

Cyril came then to Elizabeth.

She was standing at the end of the big desk, staring down at the cover Flemming had placed over it, seeing in spite of herself the great hulk that had lain there, with the spreading bloodstains below it. And the small wooden monkeys.

Cyril put his hand upon her own.

"Look here, Elizabeth, tell me again exactly what Dakin said before he died. Word for word, as nearly as you can remember it."

She did so slowly, staring at the desk and the chair beside it, remembering too well that grasp upon her wrist, the voices in the hall, the pounding on the door, the gasping difficult words Robert's clumsy lips uttered.

When she finished Cyril said nothing for a moment. The house was very still. If the police, at Friker's orders, were actually searching for the gun, for the helium reports, for three small wooden monkeys, then she heard nothing of that search. At last Cyril said, "All right. Listen, Elizabeth, there's something else I want to say. Do you remember the night in the garden of the hotel in Montego Bay—when we were talking—there above the sea . . ."

How well she remembered!

"Yes."

"You said," said Cyril, "that you didn't know, two years ago, that love was so important. Do you remember that?"

"Yes, Cyril," her voice was almost a whisper.

"Well, then—don't forget it now. That's all I wanted to say."

He turned and without another word walked out of the room, his footsteps gradually growing less distinct as he went down the hall.

She stood there for a few moments, her fingertips pressed against the top of the desk.

Remember that love is important. Remember . . .

At last the silence, and the indescribably ominous quality in that silence, as if the house itself waited for what? she wondered) roused her from thought. She turned away and walked slowly toward the hall. As she reached it, Ruth came quickly out of Dyke's room, closing the door hard behind her; from where she stood in the doorway Elizabeth caught a glimpse of Ruth's purposeful face, pale in the shadows of the hall, her frowning, black eyebrows. She came toward Elizabeth, but did not seem to see her—so intent was she on some inward thought. There was purpose in every line of her figure; intention in the way she turned quickly into her own room and closed the door. In the silence Elizabeth distinctly heard her key turn in the lock.

It struck Elizabeth, then, merely as something unexpected, a little extraordinary. Locking herself in her room in broad daylight with police in the house.

She went slowly downstairs.

Ruth had inherited everything, then; not Dyke. She felt no bitterness for herself; she hadn't wanted Robert Dakin's money; she had plenty of her own and the memory of her life with him was so bitter and so painful that she only wanted to conquer that memory, certainly to have nothing to remind her of it. Besides, he had belonged really to Charmian and Ruth and Dyke. Not to her. But to Dyke it was the end of all his hopes and expectations.

Had Ruth known she was to inherit? She had said she didn't know it. But if she had, there was a motive at least as powerful as revenge. Didn't people usually kill for money? Or in a storm of rage or hatred?

But again she thought of the impression of sincerity she had had when Ruth talked to her. "Don't you see," Ruth had said painfully, as if the words were wrenched from her very heart, "don't you see I might have been with him when he died."

She went on slowly down the stairs. No one was in the hall but the voice of the inspector came from Charlie's little room under the stairs. And there was something trivial, all but forgotten, which now she must tell him. Cyril's mention of the hotel—obscurely, only because it happened the same night—had reminded her of it, and that was the ladder which, the night before Robert had been murdered, she had seen leaning against the house.

Friker put down the telephone as she entered. "Come in, Madam. Let me give you a chair." There was a faint small triumph about him. She looked at him, noting it, and he explained, "It may interest you, Madam, to know we have news of the gun that killed Major Dakin. I advertised last night in the papers, offering a reward—and immunity, naturally—for any information about a revolver like the one that killed your husband. And I now have had a telephone from Kingston. The man who procured the gun is on his way here to identify the person for whom he procured it, on the morning of the day which Miss Reddington claims she spent shopping in Kingston and driving to Montego Bay." He didn't rub his hands together; he didn't quite smile. But he sat down in Charlie's swivel chair, made a tent with his fingertips and said, "Well, now, you came to tell me something."

She recalled her purpose almost with a start. And told him swiftly. "And the ladder was gone the next morning," she added. "I remember that because an electrician came to repair the aerial for the wireless and they—he and the gardener and even Leech were looking for the ladder. It belonged in the tool shed, I think."

He looked at her with that hard, brilliant gaze that, in moments when he was thinking deeply, was curiously blank, like a wall. Then he questioned her briefly, said, "Wait here a moment, please," went away and after five or ten minutes returned.

"Madam is right. The ladder belonged in the tool shed; the gardener was using it when he trimmed the vines above the doorway; he left it out inadvertently and the next morning it was gone. No one saw it until it was found by one of our police—as I've told you, in the shrubs in the ravine. Madam, think well; is there anything else? Remember that if you are innocent of this murder, anything you can tell me may help you."

If she was innocent! He said, "Think back, Madam. You say you saw no one after the murder. Did you see anyone—or hear anyone's voice before the murder . . ." He stopped short; his eyes bright and alert. "I see, you did hear someone . . ."

It was exactly then that, for the first time since it happened, she remembered that brief, scarcely tangible experience on the balcony—she had thought someone was below her in the darkness; it had sounded as if someone were dragging something across the grass. Something heavy, that slithered along. A ladder? But there was nothing definite, no voice, no figure, only that sliding sound.

But she told him that, too; quickly.

She could not read his expression; she had no way of knowing what he thought. He rose and said,

"Thank you, Madam," and bowed her out of the room.

Dyke stood in the hall. Charmian was just going upstairs, for Elizabeth heard the faint little rustle of silk. Had either of them heard what she told the detective? But it didn't matter. And Dyke said abruptly, "Elizabeth, will you come into the library? I want to talk to you."

He closed the door behind them and smiled suddenly at her with all the charm, all the warmth, all the youth and tenderness and appeal that she had known and remembered.

"Elizabeth," he said directly, "I've lost everything on account of you; but I don't care. I don't regret anything. All I want is you. And the promise you gave me . . ."

He fumbled in an inside coat pocket and drew out a letter. A letter on this gray stationery; a letter with her own handwriting on it.

"Dyke, let me have it."

"I want to read it to you, dearest. Listen. You began, 'Dear Dyke.' " He read it slowly, pausing as if to let every phrase and every word sink into her heart. "You said: 'I don't know what to do; my marriage was a mistake. I think our silly quarrel, yours and mine, was a dreadful mistake, too, Dyke; I have regretted it many times—everything I said to you. I married him too soon; I didn't know that he was like this. He's getting much worse—so much worse, I can't bear it any longer. I'm writing because you will know and

216

understand and perhaps help me. I don't know what to do but I must do something; anything to end it.' You signed it then, darling. 'Elizabeth.' And you added a postscript. You said, 'Please come.' " Dyke folded the letter, watching her with that bright warm look. "So I came," he said.

"I—I ought not to have written to you. I was at my wit's end. I didn't know where to turn. I needed someone who—who knew him and me. I can't excuse myself, I know; and when you came you were so . . ."

"So what?" said Dyke, his smile fixed, his eyes bright and demanding.

"So—so different," whispered Elizabeth. "Not—as I remembered you."

He laughed a little, almost gaily, except that it was so deliberate. "So the little girl's dream prince turned out to be human," he said. "Well, I'm sorry, my dear, but you sent for me, and I came. You cost me all that money; that's why he gave it to Ruth. You let him see you still loved me."

"No, no, Dyke."

"And he gave it to Ruth. Well, my dear, this is one debt you're going to pay. And if you have any notion that now you've fallen in love with this Englishman, forget it. He doesn't want you. He made it clear last night that he meant nothing. He's leaving Jamaica— he's going to England as soon as he can."

"He's going to war."

Dyke shrugged. "At any rate, he's going out of your life. I do want you and I love you. With all my heart,

217

darling . . ." He put his arms around her. His voice had become warm and reassuring again; he said tenderly, "You love me, dear. You won't let me down just when I've had a blow like this. Losing everything I've been brought up to expect. I don't reproach you for that. But you can't let me down. Now."

"Dyke, give me my letter."

"I wouldn't part with it for anything in the world." There was the pleasantest little laugh in his voice.

And all at once it seemed to Elizabeth that a bright and charming mask dropped away from his face. It was as if she saw that mask fall. And he knew that she saw it. For he laughed a little again softly. His bright eyes still smiled, yet something ugly and cold peered out of them.

"All right, Elizabeth; if you must have the truth. I'm not going to give you this letter. I'm not going to destroy it. And you're going to be a sensible girl. Do you understand me?"

After a moment she said stiffly, "I was right then, two years ago, when I said you were a fortune hunter."

He said softly, still smiling, "It's an interesting fact that a murder case can be reopened years afterward. You do understand me, don't you?"

"I understand that you are threatening me with this letter. That you don't love me; you never have. But you want money . . ."

"I've lost a great deal of money," said Dyke. "And I hope to keep this letter always. Sorry to be so melodramatic, my dear, but it really is time we understood each other."

It was just then that Flemming knocked gently and opened the door. His long face was ashen. He cried shakenly, "Madam, Leech is dead. They've just found him."

"Dead!" said Dyke.

Flemming's pale blue eyes were filled with horror.

"Murdered," he said. "This morning. While the nurse was resting. Smothered with his own pillow."

23

LEECH'S MURDER was almost incredibly simple, and there was no evidence and no clue leading to the murderer.

The circumstances of it were clear—too clear.

The old man had seemed better and stronger and likely to return to consciousness. The nurse had left him to take a rest; there had been no reason for him to believe that the old butler was in danger. He had stayed with him all night, had talked to Cyril when he came, briefly, to inquire, and about nine in the morning had gone to sleep in Flemming's room at a little distance down the hall. The other servants had all been up and about their work, so the servants' wing, except for the butler and the nurse, was deserted. And when the nurse awoke and returned to his patient about noon, Leech was dead; smothered quietly —because the old man was still unconscious—and efficiently.

No one had seen anyone come and go from the servants' wing. There was a back stairway, connecting with the main part of the house. The butler's room was beside it, facilitating that murderous and easy approach. The servants' wing was on the ground floor and there was an open window in Leech's room and an outside door at the end of a near-by passage. It had been fiendishly simple in conception and easy to accomplish.

And there were no clues.

The man who had been sent to take care of Leech—having been an accredited nurse—was in the employ of the inspector, placed there to keep his eyes and ears open. And he knew nothing.

Friker undertook to question the servants, to question everybody; it was a long-drawn-out task which netted him nothing.

There was again the commotion of arriving police, searching house and grounds under Friker's orders, of an ambulance drawing up at the back door; of inquiry. Elizabeth, standing at the windows of the morning room, saw the long ambulance round the curve of the driveway and disappear into the fog.

It was late afternoon before the commotion began to die away. It seemed to Elizabeth, indeed, that all at once a spell had been put upon it, and the house grew quiet again.

She stood at the window in the morning room, staring out at the gray fog that pressed against the glass. The room was—or had been, after the inspector finished questioning her about Leech—an oasis of calm,

221

so far from the rest of the house that she could see and hear as little as possible of all that ugly turmoil.

She hadn't known anything; it was queer that she had, really, known so little of the old man who had served her so well, and who had been so genuinely kind. She knew that he had no family and that he had worked for Robert Dakin many years; that when Robert Dakin retired from active participation in business he had brought Leech from America to England and thence to Jamaica with him. She knew he had rheumatism and that he liked to go fishing along the blue inlets on his days off. That was all.

Ruth was questioned, and Charmian who might be expected to know more of Leech than any of them, and Dyke. All of them, in fact, were questioned. She had seen Cyril leaving the library where, again, Friker conducted his interviews. Ruth had gone straight back to her room after lunch—cooked and served by a demoralized staff and constantly interrupted by the police inquiry—and had again locked herself in.

It was almost a foregone conclusion that Leech's murder was a result of, or at least in some way connected with, Robert Dakin's murder. He must have known something that, on reflection, the murderer realized would be dangerous knowledge. Therefore, before he became conscious and could tell that damaging fact, he was murdered. There wasn't any other tenable theory.

Another car started outside; she heard the throb of

the engine and opened the long French doors and went out upon the wet terrace.

Fog lay heavily everywhere and touched her cheeks with wet fingers and clustered in little silver beads on her hair. It was a police car leaving. She thought she saw Friker sitting in it beside the driver. Then it, too, rounded the curve below the royal palms and passed beyond the wall and into the gray wreaths of fog.

She wondered what, if any, conclusion they had reached. And wondered too, all at once, if they had found the gun Charlie had said was gone from the steel filing cabinet.

And then she thought again with horror of the simple and easy fashion of Leech's murder. As simple, as easy as her own would have been.

The fog pressed nearer, and early dusk was coming on. The wet tiles of the terrace were cold through her slippers. She turned and went into the house and instantly its silence, its brooding air of waiting, enclosed her again.

Where had Cyril gone and when? She had had only that one glimpse of him since the news of Leech's murder; he had said nothing, had scarcely glanced at her. What was Ruth doing, locked away in her room?

It struck her suddenly that all of the police must have gone. Otherwise the house would not be so still. But surely one or two had remained—for their protection, if nothing else.

One lamp was lighted in the big room that was actually, in its spaciousness and the wide outlook from the open jalousies of the many windows and doors, more like a veranda than a room. She turned on the table lamp and one or two others but still it seemed shadowy and dark. The light rattan and wicker chairs and tables, the thin, bright cushions, all designed for coolness, seemed, that day, gloomy and cold; the hard and—in that warm, moist climate—protective coats of varnish over everything that could be varnished had dismal highlights. She sat down and lighted a cigarette.

It was no good thinking of Dyke. It was no good telling herself she had been a fool; asking herself how she could have been so blind.

Would her letter to Dyke really weigh as heavily against her with the inspector as Dyke told her it would? It was too faint a hope that it would not. Anyone could have murdered Leech. Owing to the rather long period of time during which he was left alone, as well as the difficulty of establishing the exact time of his death, no one in the house, herself included, had an alibi.

And in spite of the case the inspector had built up against Ruth, in spite of his rather pleasant and candid-appearing manner of telling her, Elizabeth, of that case, still there was no dodging the fact that when all was said and done there was a far stronger case against Elizabeth herself as the murderer of Robert Dakin than against anyone else.

No, she couldn't dismiss the importance of the letter she had written Dyke, in Friker's hands. Read

before a jury. What couldn't a prosecuting attorney—
the prosecutor for the Crown; wasn't that his title—
make of it?

She put out her cigarette jerkily and instantly
lighted another.

There was nothing to do but wait. She rose again
and went restlessly to the windows.

In her heart—even realizing as she did that if Ruth
had not murdered Robert then she herself became
again the only real suspect—she still could not accept
the theory the inspector had suggested. Had called,
she remembered too clearly, an alternative.

Ruth's look of shock and grief; the things she had
said, the things she had done had had an irrefutable
stamp of sincerity. Ruth was not an actress; she was
not innately dramatic—as, for instance, Charmian
was, so that you sensed it at once.

It was true that Ruth, almost alone, profited by
Robert's death. Ruth and herself, for there were the
emeralds, willed to her; the two houses for her use.
But Dyke had thought he was to profit.

Dyke? But Dyke had a supported alibi; it blocked
off instantly any avenue of suspicion.

Someone was coming along the passage leading to
the big, many-windowed room. She whirled around
sharply, nails digging into her palms. Who—but it
could only be Charmain or Ruth or . . .

It was Ruth. She came in quickly, said, "Elizabeth
—oh, it's you," and came toward her. She held an
envelope in her hand and was extremely pale above

her neat black gown. She said rather nervously, "Have you seen Charlie anywhere? He's not in his room."

"No. No one has been here. Ruth, have all the police gone? Is there any news at all?"

Ruth said, "I don't know. Except"—she hesitated, came quite close to Elizabeth and took a long breath and said abruptly—"it's queer, Elizabeth. Dyke told me this morning that you wanted to leave Robert. If you had told me that . . ." she stopped again and seemed to follow some obscure train of thought for a moment, and then shook her smooth black head. "Yet it wouldn't have made much difference, perhaps. Except I wouldn't have done what I did. I wouldn't have been responsible for his murder."

"His . . ." Elizabeth caught her breath. "Ruth, what are you saying? What do you mean?"

Ruth tapped the envelope she carried with the white fingers of her other hand and watched Elizabeth with somber dark eyes.

"Just what I say," she said after a moment. "You see, Elizabeth, I—I wanted your marriage with Robert annulled."

It was perhaps the last thing she would have expected Ruth to say.

"Annulled!" she cried. "But it was a perfectly legal marriage! You don't mean that . . ."

"Oh, yes," said Ruth with a queer effect of weariness. "It could have been annulled. The whole thing, his divorce from Charmian and your marriage, could

226

have been set aside if there had been proof of collusion. Collusion between him and Charmian, I mean, when they agreed to seek a divorce and did so. Charmian got the divorce; but the evidence was supplied. It is in many divorces. But in this case I had proof of collusion. Letters. I intended to supply that proof."

But it made no sense. Elizabeth said slowly, "I don't understand you, Ruth. I don't see what you would have gained by it."

It was never possible to read Ruth's face; it was less so now. She said coolly, "Don't you, Elizabeth? Look in that mirror behind you."

She didn't move. And Ruth went on, "You see, Elizabeth, I was beginning to believe, after two years during which I had not seen Robert and he had not tried to see me, that you were a much more formidable rival than—than Charmian had ever been. Do you understand now? I had to get rid of you. Even if it meant that his marriage to Charmian would be automatically reinstated. He didn't love Charmian, and I knew it. But you—that was different."

There was another pause.

"But he didn't love me," Elizabeth said at last. "He married me—for any number of reasons, perhaps. But not for love."

"You are young—he wanted a wife like you. He was vain and he had his pride," said Ruth as a mere statement of fact.

"But he didn't love me," said Elizabeth again.

Ruth nodded. "I know that now. But I didn't then.

227

So I came prepared to provide the evidence of collusion; to see that Charmian's divorce and your marriage were set aside. Amicably, quietly—there are ways. If she wanted to divorce him again later—you see, then he would be free again . . ." She stopped. "Oh, you are such a child, Elizabeth! Don't stare at me like that. I tell you I loved him. I'd loved him for years. I wanted—I wanted marriage. In the end. When, if you must hear the last ugly truth, when I'd got rid of Charmian again. As I did once before. I'm not getting any younger. He's always been the only man—the only thing in all the world that mattered to me. Well, I—I wanted him." She put up her head defiantly, her great, dark eyes daring Elizabeth to speak. "I wanted him. And I intended to have him. I thought he loved you for your—youth and your beauty. I thought if I could end your marriage to him, even if only by reinstating his marriage to Charmian, I could in the end get him back again. In a little time Charmian could get another divorce if she wanted to, as I was sure she would want to. And by that time he would have forgotten you; he would need me. And I"—said Ruth harshly, "would be there. Do you understand?"

She was trembling. Elizabeth saw it. She said, "I—I'm sorry."

"Luckily," said Ruth, "I found a means I thought I could use to persuade Charmian; a technicality which her lawyer had overlooked at the time of the divorce. By Texas law, you see, Charmian could have had a share of all the money he made during the time when she was his wife.

"In Texas property is held jointly by husband and wife; community property, it is called. If, at the time of a divorce, they don't arrive at a settlement themselves the court may make a disposal of money between the husband and wife; this includes all money and property they possess at the time the marriage ends, except real estate.

"Charmian got her divorce in Europe; she didn't know, somehow, about Texas law, and neither, apparently, did her lawyer here know it. So she had no share in Robert's money. But if she could be persuaded to admit collusion; to seek to have the divorce set aside and her marriage to Robert reinstated—then, if she sought another divorce, this time in Texas, she could legally claim and (because they had been married so long and Robert had made so much money during that time) almost certainly receive a really big sum of money. She could, in case of a second divorce, be a very rich woman." She stopped and again took a long breath. "You see, I thought I had it all arranged. I—I'm good, you know, at business; everyone has always said so. I can outthink my opponents; I can plan their next move and then my own. This time—I failed."

A hundred things came to Elizabeth's tongue; yet she could only stand there, as if frozen, helpless, unable to move or speak.

Ruth thrust her white, strong hand into the bosom

of her dress. She pulled out a handkerchief, knotted. She said, "The emeralds are here. I brought them to you, Elizabeth. I don't want them. Besides, they are yours now. And I—look . . ." clasping the envelope closer she opened the handkerchief. There were the emeralds and there was also, in the handkerchief, almost hidden with the sleepy green fire of the necklace, the small wooden image of three monkeys.

Elizabeth thought she spoke, but she couldn't have. For Ruth went on abruptly, "I took them from Dyke's room last night; he'd hidden them and I found them; while he was in Kirby's room—you were there, too. I took the monkeys and I know now all about them. I—remembered." She paused sharply; then turned her head very slowly toward the door.

Involuntarily, Elizabeth followed her look. There was nothing there. No sound. The whole house was quiet—almost breathlessly quiet. Waiting? Then for what? But that was nonsense; fancy engendered by the fog outside—the clustered shadows inside.

Ruth's fingers tightened on the envelope. She opened her lips to speak, closed them, listened again. And said, "I know the whole story, Elizabeth. I've told you part of it; I will tell you more later. But I— I'm not going to tell Friker. There's a reason. Elizabeth—will you do something for me? It's—important." One hand closed convulsively on the incongruous little heap. Emeralds worth a fortune, a linen handkerchief; three shabby little wooden monkeys. The other pushed the envelope into Elizabeth's own

230

hand. "Will you and Charlie—he'll be here in a minute—take this letter and put it in the safe? I—you see, you are wearing a jacket. You can hide it—under your jacket. So no one will see. No one but Charlie will know. Then, when you've done that, come back to me."

24

THE ENVELOPE was in her hand. It was soft gray, thin, of the house stationery with which the guest rooms were supplied. It felt as if there were several folded sheets inside it and it was sealed with no address.

"Please do it, Elizabeth. I wouldn't ask you to if—but no one would suspect that I had given it to you . . ."

"What is it?"

Ruth met her gaze openly.

"It's something I want Charlie to put in the safe. That's all. And I want you to go with him to make sure it is put in the safe and—and because I want him to know that you know about it." Again she glanced over her shoulder. "Do you understand? I trust Charlie, but . . ." Someone was coming along the passage and her white strong hands made a quick motion toward each other almost in supplication. "Here he comes now. No one but Charlie will know you have it," she said. "Put it under your jacket."

232

She came so near that Elizabeth could see the blue vein throbbing on her white temple and thrust the envelope under Elizabeth's arm, below the loose, light gray jacket of her dress. "There, you see; hold it with the pressure of your arm. Like that. I wouldn't ask you to do it if it were not so important. And it— believe me: it is dangerous to me; but it is not dangerous to you."

She never knew why she did it; perhaps it was the urgency in Ruth's eyes and face and beseeching hands. Perhaps it was the slightness of the errand. To walk upstairs with Charlie Hawes and watch him put an envelope in the safe. No more than that.

Charlie, his narrow face ghostly in the shadow, had stopped in the doorway, his eyes on Ruth. "You asked me to come in ten minutes," he began irresolutely.

"Yes. Mrs. Dakin has a letter of mine you are to put in the safe. She'll—go with you."

Charlie shrugged. His rabbit face was pale and uneasy but, Elizabeth thought, incurious. "All right," he said, and turned into the corridor and she followed him, leaving Ruth there in the morning room with her somber dark eyes watching, and one hand still clasping a wrinkled little handkerchief which held the monkeys and the emeralds in that strange juxtaposition.

Charlie hurried ahead of her along the corridor; there was no one else there and no one in the hall.

It was curious how suddenly deserted the place was. She glanced up the stairway indecisively when they

233

reached it, holding her arm tight against her so the envelope would not slip. Dangerous to Ruth; not dangerous to her. *But if Ruth knew the whole story as she said, why didn't she go to the police with it?*

But Charlie was there still ahead of her, sliding quickly up the stairway and keeping close to the shadowy wall. She started up after him. It was very dark in the hall above; an early gray twilight was already falling. She would turn on the hall light when she reached the top of the steps. She must have been halfway up the stairs, just at the curve, with the empty shadowy hall below her, when the envelope slipped and, before she could catch it, slithered through the spokes of the stair railing and out of sight into the hall below.

It gave her the queerest kind of start; that sliding letter, the futile clutch she made for it, the sight of its falling into the shadows below.

But instantly she turned and ran down the steps and the letter lay, a patch of white, on the floor where it had fallen. She ran to it and snatched it and oddly hurried, as if pursued where no one was there to pursue, turned again toward the stairs. And thought suddenly, Exactly what has Ruth written in this letter that I hold in my hand; why shouldn't I open it and read it? What was a convention when danger lay like a trap concealed in that silent and shadowy house?

She stopped. Probably she would have opened the letter, in spite of Ruth's reassurances, then and there. But Charlie leaned over the railing. His face was

234

ghostly against the murky shadows above. His eyes were suspicious. "What happened? I thought you were coming," he said. And waited, eyes alert and watchful while she went up the steps and joined him. This time he did not go ahead of her but remained close beside her.

At the curve again she glanced downward and had a quick impression that, just then, someone—something moved back into the cavernous shadows of the dark dining room. But it wasn't possible. No one had been there. No one would jerk back like that, suddenly, silently, so it was only an impression of white face, a faint rustle of motion, a deeper shadow among those other shadows. No one had been there; she told herself that. And went with Charlie, quickly, along the hall to the study.

He went at once to the safe, moved the dials expertly and looked at her. "Well," he said, eyes little and nervous. "Give me the letter."

She glanced at the door. The house was as quiet as if there was no one in it but herself and Charlie Hawes.

"Well," he said again, fretfully.

She gave him the envelope. He turned it over.

"What is it? There's nothing written on it."

"I don't know," she said. "Just—just put it in the safe. That's all."

He glanced at her again, rather sharply; below his rabbity, timorous exterior Charlie was no fool. But he thrust the envelope inside the safe, closed the door quickly and twirled the dials. And without another word or look hurried out of the room.

He met someone in the hall; there was the murmur of voices, then Dyke came hurriedly into the room.

"Elizabeth! Charlie said you were here. I've been looking for you. It's—it's important."

He too, as Ruth had done, glanced over his shoulder and then came closer to her; there was an air of haste and urgency about him as if time pressed. He said quickly, "Listen, Elizabeth. You've been thinking pretty harsh things of me. Well, I'm going to show you I'm not such a bad fellow after all. I'm going to give you a chance to see Cyril."

"See—what do you mean?"

"Friker found the helium papers among Cyril's things. Cyril's leaving—I don't know how or why. But he's got to get away, he says. The police have gone except for a couple Friker left here for our own protection. Cyril wants to see you before he goes. He's waiting in the ravine below the garden. He said to hurry." He paused and said slowly, "I promised him to bring you to him. I want you to remember that, Elizabeth. And credit me with it. The police are searching for him in Montego Bay now. No one but me knows he's still on the grounds."

That was, then, why Friker had gone. That and to see the man who was to arrive from Kingston; to be questioned about the revolver. She had forgotten that.

Dyke said, "I told him I'd bring you. He says he's
236

got to see you before he goes. It's nothing to me; I only wanted to prove to you that I—wasn't so bad. Shall I tell him you won't come?"

"I'll go," she said, thinking, just then, only of Cyril. Dyke turned and followed her along the hall and down the stairs. This time no one moved in the cavernous shadows beyond the dining-room door.

Dyke opened the coat closet, pulled out a thin rubber rain cape and put it around her shoulders. He took out a coat for himself. And suddenly an inner warning voice said, but this is not safe; murder is at large. The murderer might be Dyke, it might be anyone. She hesitated, remembering Robert Dakin, remembering the old butler, remembering a pillow, smothering and hot across her face. But that attack had failed. And Cyril was waiting for her in the ravine. And then all at once she remembered that she would be safe with Dyke and why. Ironically Robert Dakin's own contemptuous words rang again in her ears and reminded her. "I'm his bank roll," Robert had said. Dyke wanted money and hoped to secure it through her; rather obviously, it seemed to her all at once, Dyke was trying to reinstate himself in her good graces by taking her to Cyril. No, she would be safe with Dyke.

And Cyril would have come to her if she needed him. The helium papers—everything else could wait; nothing else really mattered. Except that Cyril had sent for her.

But Ruth was in the morning room, waiting, too.

Ruth with that tragic white face; Ruth, ready to tell her the thing she knew of the monkeys.

"This way," said Elizabeth, and pulled the cape around her and turned toward the corridor. Dyke said something impatient but followed her. Their footsteps sounded loud along the floor of the corridor. And when they reached the morning room, Ruth was gone.

Elizabeth stopped short. The library door had been open, the drawing-room door also; she had seen no one in either room. And if Ruth had been in Charlie's small room under the stairs she would have heard them come, would have spoken.

"What is it? What are you waiting for? Come along."

Dyke was opening the door onto the terrace. She felt a warm mist on her face. It was later than she had thought. The fog was heavier than ever; it was difficult to see objects clearly at a distance of ten or fifteen feet; tall objects loomed out of the fog like thick black ghosts and then as you neared them turned into trees.

They were crossing the lawn; Dyke hurrying, making her hurry. It was like a wilderness. So bewildering that he made a mistake in direction and brought up at some shrubs, heavy and drooping and wet, instead of the garden path, and had to take a bearing from there and presently reached the great drooping banyan tree and the steps that led into the garden.

No one was about; no figure loomed out of the fog

238

and became a man; no voice spoke to them. They went along the turf path through the garden, toward the break in the wall and in the hedge where the path entered the ravine.

Still nothing moved in that fog. It was as if only she and Dyke were left in all the world. And Cyril, waiting for her.

When Dyke spoke his voice was hushed and unreal, as ghostly as that shrouded garden.

"I'll go ahead," he said. "It's not much further. Look out—the path's slippery." He went ahead.

The path was slippery. The turf ended as they passed beyond the garden wall and the path became abruptly uneven, with small stones and slippery wet leaves that slid from under her feet. It was irregular, too; turning constantly among the entangled growth. Wet leaves brushed her hand; a branch touched her face. The path turned again ahead of her and so did Dyke.

It was much darker in the ravine with the heavy foliage of the trees and of the thick shrubs crowding along the path, shutting out what light there was. Very dark, with the fog heavier.

She must hurry. When she rounded the next curve of the path, Dyke's dark shoulders loomed in the mist much farther ahead.

She was bewildered and had lost her sense of direction. It seemed to her that the path suddenly grew narrower, so she had almost to force her way through

239

the wildly growing thickets in order to keep the dark, tall figure ahead of her in sight.

Again Dyke disappeared beyond a fog-enshrouded mangrove thicket. She followed hurriedly, slipped on the path that was almost no path now, grasped out at thick foliage and wild vines which shook a cold little shower on her face, righted herself, and started again to follow Dyke.

It was perhaps five steps further on that it seemed to her that the height and shape of those dark shoulders had altered. Had become—she stopped dead still —had become someone else. Or no one. For instantly whatever—whoever she was following was gone, disappeared completely into the fog.

She didn't move for a moment. Where was Dyke— where had he gone—didn't he know she was not with him?

And then she saw that she had lost the path; she was completely surrounded by unknown shapes, half-seen in the darkness and fog. Where was the path? Off at the right? Where, then?

And where was Dyke?

She turned and pushed her way toward, she thought, the path. How had she gone so far from it? How had she let herself become so confused? Moments passed while she groped among the wet lush foliage. Dyke must come back for her. She would hear his call any instant. She even tried to call to him, but her voice was breathless, curiously muffled by the fog, and yet it seemed strangely loud in that stillness.

240

The fog was everywhere, pressing in upon her, starting out inexorably from every shadow—every lush thicket—if she tried again to call out, if she screamed even, it would be lost against that muffling enveloping gray blanket.

Presently she told herself that she must stop and think. She must listen. The terror that had reached like gray tentacles out of the fog to clutch at her was a thing of fancy, nothing else. Surely she would hear Dyke's footsteps—something.

But there was nothing. No sound of footsteps, no voice calling her. Nothing at all. Except that all at once somewhere in the fog quite near her there was a sound. A dreadful sound, for someone, somewhere, screamed. It was a scream that rose thin and sharp and horrible, cutting those muffling veils in a very anguish of terror, and then abruptly stopped.

Stopped because it was drowned by another sound and that was a revolver shot.

The fog held the sound to the earth, among the trees, pushing it back and forth relentlessly among the gray shapes around her. But it was quite near. She turned and fought her way through brush, through shapes that rose out of the night and the fog.

Certainly she had no thought of finding the path again, but she did. Almost immediately she came upon it; she turned to the left thinking, if she thought anything, that that would take her back to the garden and out of that horror-charged ravine.

It did lead toward the garden; but she had fumbled

her way only a few steps and around a curve when she came upon the thing that lay there in the path. A dark heap, dreadfully limp, black in that fog, face downward.

It was Ruth.

She saw that.

And then she saw or perhaps only felt, the slight, shaking motion of the glossy, wet leaves of a shrub at the edge of the path just beyond Ruth's body; it loomed only a little out of the fog. But the thick green foliage trembled and there was no wind. There was nothing in that ravine but fog and Ruth, dead on the path, and that moving branch not ten feet away.

25

It moved again.

Someone far above, distant in the fog, shouted to someone else. It was as far away just then as if it were in another world.

The dark shadow away back of that wet, lush, green curtain seemed to gather itself together and have form.

And Elizabeth gave one despairing glance at the thing that lay in the path and fled. Into the thick, wild brush again, away from that path and the moving branch and into blurred shapes of trees and brush that rose out of the dusk and clutched at her as if with fingers. Stones and wet leaf mold slid under her feet. She found herself in a little thicket and stopped to listen.

It wasn't possible; but it was true.

Ruth was dead. Ruth was murdered. And whoever murdered Ruth had stood behind that leafy curtain and watched Elizabeth. Was the murderer following her? Now?

She was panting. Her own pulses were drumming in her ears. She held her breath to listen. And heard a stone slide a little—cautiously, not far from her.

And then began that stealthy, horrible stalking. From black shrub to black shrub, taking care lest a twig slip below one's foot, lest a protruding branch catch at one's skirt—listening always for a twig to snap below another foot, for the rustle of a body slipping between wet, thick foliage.

It was like any hunt, except that Elizabeth was being hunted. By whom? she kept thinking in some part of her mind. Dyke? Charmian? Charlie? Once, even, fantastically, she thought of Flemming. Yet there was something inhuman, something savage and feral about that stealthy, dogged pursuit.

Once or twice she heard shouts, too distant, too far away. They meant only that someone at the house had heard the shot, muffled though it was by fog and distance. That perhaps up there a search was being made.

But they could never find her in time, never find the thing that crept relentlessly after her, betraying itself by such small signs. Again there was a soft rustle as a branch slipped back into place when it was released by a body that moved away. She heard that and again cautiously, with infinite stealth, she crept to another little thicket of brush and crouched in its shadows. And listened.

244

She had no way of knowing who followed her. She only knew it was murder, quite determined, and quite ruthless.

Once she thought of what Charlie had said about the gun that was lost. "Was it loaded?" he had been asked. And had refused to answer.

And then something rustled furtively, like the passage of a small animal, in the black little covert through which she had just come and she moved again, clinging to the trunks of trees, finding her way into another shadow. If she screamed as Ruth had screamed, they could not find her in time.

She was this time in a twisted thicket of mangroves, and it made a sort of recess around her, so small and close that branches pressed tight around her and if she moved any of them, moving too, would betray her. She crouched down a little so her face would not show white in the dusk and again listened.

And a branch snapped quite close. She held her breath and something moved on the other side of the screening, thick, tropical foliage. Cautious footsteps went on, passed the tree. And then came back.

The sounds were less cautious. A branch was pushed aside and Elizabeth saw it spring back into place. There was another footstep and then pressure against the branches that shielded her. And all at once something like a hand, gloved and dark, came gliding through the thick branches toward her, came almost to her arm, went past it, touched the tree and came back, slowly, deliberately searching. And as it came nearer she turned with a sob in her throat, and, casting aside all attempt of concealment, ran—stumbling, blundering, sobbing into the surrounding thickets with something like a dreadful echo crashing through the tangled growth behind her.

She came out unexpectedly on the path again; there was no time to consider; she turned again to the left and ran through fog and all at once, without any warning, came around a curve and brought up against a man also running. He caught her quickly to keep his balance and her own, held her, looked down through the dusk and cried, "Elizabeth—" It was Cyril. "What's happened? Elizabeth . . ."

She clung to him, speechless. He cried,

"Was that a shot? A while ago, I mean?" he caught her tight in his arms. "What's happened?"

"Cyril, where were you? Dyke told me you were in the ravine, waiting for me . . ."

Her voice was shrill and taut; he replied rapidly, "I've been in town; I just got back—I was strolling around the grounds when I heard the shot. I didn't know where—what—the fog . . ." He broke off. "Elizabeth, tell me . . ."

"Someone—Ruth . . ." All at once she was sobbing.

"What do you mean? Quick. Elizabeth—no one's here now . . ."

"Cyril, she's dead. And whoever killed her is back there. Coming. Through the brush—*listen* . . ." She turned in his arms to look back into the fog. But nothing came from it, and there were no sounds now from that mask of foliage and gray shadow. No sounds except that suddenly, running heavily along the path from the garden, were two policemen. They came out of the fog quickly, two solid uniformed figures.

"What's gone wrong here? What was that shot?" They took Cyril by the arm and they caught her, too, and pulled her away from Cyril and when she tried to tell them that Ruth was dead—murdered—and that the murderer had been there and had slipped stealthily away into the fog and dusk when Cyril found her, they scarcely listened, it seemed to her, but shouted back orders to another policeman who came out of the fog in their wake.

The third had his revolver in his hand. So had the first two, but she hadn't noticed it till then. Cyril's face was a pale oval in the dusk. The policemen's blue helmets looked sharply black. Cyril said, "Hold on, Elizabeth. Steady."

And two policemen were running along the path again—around a curve and out of sight—toward—why, toward Ruth, of course. There was a sharp silence; they had found her, then. And her murderer had vanished into the green, wet mask of leaves, dripping with mist, which again merely observed and kept its secret.

At last one of the policemen came hurrying back. He had now an electric torch and its pale rays reflected themselves in glistening lights against wet leaves. He spoke briefly to the policeman who guarded them, turned, paying no attention to Cyril's sharp inquiry, and hurried off into the fog again.

"Right about, please," said the policeman who remained, holding his revolver ready in his hand. "Along the path, if you please. We'll go back to the house . . ."

"But the woman that was shot—" cried Cyril. "Whoever killed her was here a few moments ago and . . ."

"You heard me."

It was a queer procession, Cyril first—shoulders black in the dusk ahead of her as Dyke's had been (where was Dyke?). Herself next, then the policeman. They were not far, after all, from the entrance to the garden.

That was queer, too; she felt as if she had been in an uncharted wilderness. With only fog and murder and—what had Cyril said? Steady, there, Elizabeth. But had the murderer escaped this way, too?

They went along the garden path and up the steps and across the lawn. There were muffled voices from the ravine below which, from where she now stood, was merely a dense patch of darkness. There was a car at the steps with its lights burning and sending out short, diffused little lanes of light into the swirling gray wreaths. Lights were in the house, too.

And then they reached the door and someone opened it and the policeman behind them said, "Here they are, sir. Caught in the ravine. Not fifteen feet

248

away from the murdered woman. Miss Ruth Reddington. She was shot."

The lights were confusing. Her hair was disheveled; wet wisps clung to her face and she pushed them back and a wet leaf, caught somewhere, fluttered to the floor.

Dyke was in the hall, and Friker, and Flemming. *"Elizabeth,"* cried Dyke and came forward quickly. Cyril, standing beside her, looked so very queer—so stern and white. And Friker glanced at them and at the policeman, and said sharply, "Are you sure?"

"I didn't see her, sir. The others went ahead and looked and told me to bring these two up to the house; to deliver them to you. We heard the shot."

The door opened again and another policeman came quickly to Friker and saluted briskly.

"The woman is dead," he said. "Miss Ruth Reddington. She has been murdered." He jerked around, his eyes sought and found Cyril and Elizabeth and he said, "They did it."

"Is anyone there with the body?"

"Yes, sir. Harris. There were only the three of us; the two that were here on the grounds and I. I had discovered Mr. Kirby in town and had followed him back here in a taxicab. I dismissed the cab at the entrance to the grounds. I met his empty taxicab returning and assumed he had entered the house. I was coming along the drive when I heard the sound of the shot. The sound in the fog was very confusing. We hunted all over the grounds near the house before we concluded the shot came from the ravine, and when we reached it we found these two."

"Do you mean to say there was time after Kirby arrived and before you reached the house for him to go down to the ravine and kill the woman?"

"Yes, sir. Besides, no one else was there."

"You are sure the woman is dead?"

"Very sure," said the policeman and looked very sober, and shook a tiny shower of mist from his cap.

"Telephone headquarters. Then go down to the ravine and don't leave the woman until the men from headquarters come. When the men come, search the ravine and grounds; we can't do it until then. Now then . . ." He turned toward the library, his clear, fine-featured face sharp against the wooden paneling of the room. "You others, come in here." He looked at Flemming. "Find Mr. Hawes," he said. "And the other Mrs. Dakin and tell them I want to see them."

Flemming vanished. Dyke came to Elizabeth as if to speak to her, and Cyril quite neatly and instantly interposed himself between them, so they entered the library with Elizabeth going first, then Cyril, then Dyke. It was a small and quiet maneuver.

And then she saw a stranger sitting uneasily in the corner of the library in one of the carved, old chairs. He was smoking and had been smoking for some time, judging by the ends of cigarettes in the tray in his hand. He was thin and swarthy, with a lock of black hair across his forehead and uneasy, shifting eyes. He wore a dark suit of an exaggeratedly fashionable cut;

250

a large ring with a doubtful sapphire in it, and extraordinarily fancy shoes. He got up quickly as they entered, his uneasy eyes darting from them to Friker.

Friker nodded at him, as if to say, wait a moment; at any rate, he waited, watching them all the time with those shifting, quick eyes and smoking nervously. And Friker said, "Sit down, Mrs. Dakin. Now then—exactly what happened?"

Dyke stepped forward, "I think I can tell you something of it at any rate. Mrs. Dakin and I were in the ravine—simply walking for a little air. We didn't realize the fog was so thick; the path turned and somehow I lost Elizabeth. I called to her, but she didn't answer, and I assumed she had come back to the house, so I came back, too." He looked at Elizabeth, his eyes warm and bright. "Isn't that right, Elizabeth? I ought to have waited but I thought you'd come back."

But they had gone to meet Cyril. And she had met Cyril—but that was later. He hadn't been waiting in the ravine as Dyke said he was waiting. He had been in town and had just got back when he heard the shot. And the policeman had said he'd followed Cyril from Montego Bay to the house, dismissed the cab, walked toward the house and on the driveway heard the shot. So Cyril was not in the ravine, waiting to see her, when Dyke said he was there. Then why . . .

Dyke saw the question in her face. He came closer to her, but again Cyril moved quietly between them, this time reaching casually for an ashtray. Dyke said,

"It was mere accident that Elizabeth was in the ravine. Tell them you didn't kill her, Elizabeth."

Cyril's hand closed tight on the ashtray. His face was grim and white. "Tell them the truth, Elizabeth," he said.

"We went to the ravine to meet Cyril. Dyke said he was there and wanted me to come. It's true that Dyke and I did become separated in the fog; I didn't hear him call to me. Then after some time I heard the shot and Ruth—Ruth was in the path." Her voice wavered and Cyril, without looking at her, put his hand upon her own. "There was someone in the brush, following me. After a while I came upon the path again and I was running along it toward the garden when I met Cyril, running toward me. He didn't kill her; and I didn't."

Dyke said, "You're hysterical, Elizabeth. You've had a shock. . . ."

And Cyril said, "I was at a distant part of the grounds when I heard the shot; the fog and the dusk were confusing. I couldn't tell where the sound came from. I believe the police were searching near the house; they were equally handicapped by the fog and the dusk. I could hear their voices now and then, but it was almost impossible to see anyone or anything at a distance. It seemed to me that the sound came from the ravine or the garden. I went there and . . ."

"You were alone?"

"Until I met Mrs. Dakin, yes. But I'm telling you the truth . . ."

"Where exactly were you when you heard the sound of the shot? And why?"

"I was somewhere near the garage. I—I was simply walking because I felt like it. I had some rather interesting news I wanted to think about. Something I want to tell you, if you will permit me."

Friker lifted one fine, slender hand. "One moment, Mr. Kirby. You knew that helium-producing gas had been discovered in the Dakin oil district?"

A faint expression of surprise came into Cyril's face. "Why, yes. Major Dakin told me. But that has nothing to do with what I . . ."

"You were interested in the helium?"

"Why—naturally. Helium is scarce . . ."

"The reports brought here by Mr. Sanderson and Ruth Reddington have been found among your things; they were found just after lunch; in the lining of your large brown Gladstone, to be precise."

There was a little pause. Cyril's gray eyes were as hard as steel. "I know nothing about them. I did not take them. If they were there, Sanderson put them there."

"You were once in the Intelligence Service?"

"Yes. Long ago."

"Are you now?"

"No," said Cyril flatly and directly, "I am not. I'm in the regular army—or will be as soon as I can get back to England. Look here, I didn't take those helium reports; I don't know anything about it. But I do know why Ruth and Dyke came separately to

Montego Bay and earlier than they chose to admit. Do you want to hear the reason?"

Dyke was perfectly still. The inspector said, "Why?"

"They both wanted to see Charmian. The first Mrs. Dakin. They both went to her house out Brandon Hill way to see her; Ruth first, about three in the afternoon; Dyke later about five o'clock."

The inspector said slowly, "My friends, you embarrass me with clues. Either you, Mrs. Dakin, murdered your husband and Leech and now, with Mr. Kirby's assistance, killed Ruth Reddington. Or"—he whirled around suddenly toward Dyke and said—"or you did it."

"I didn't do it," said Dyke quickly. "You can't accuse me."

"Oh," said Friker. "Then your choice for murderer is Mrs. Dakin? Well, then, why did you take a ladder from the front of the house the *night before* Major Dakin was shot, hide it in the ravine, bring it out shortly before his murder, plant it at Ruth's window, and then almost immediately, before the murder took place—for it was not there when the police arrived—remove it again and hide it in the ravine? There is no good saying you didn't; we found your fingerprints upon it." He paused a moment.

Dyke did not speak and the expression in his face did not change. And the man in the corner came forward as if at an unseen signal from the inspector.

"That's the man I got the gun for," he said, "that

254

morning in Kingston. I was in a bar, as I told you. He came in and got to talking and—and he paid me a hundred dollars and said to be sure to get a gun for him that couldn't be traced. That's the man," he said and pointed at Dyke.

The little smile on Dyke's face was curiously fixed. He said nothing.

"It was clever of you," said the inspector, "to secure the gun that morning, before your trip to Montego Bay. This man has identified the gun that killed Major Dakin; he has now identified you. I need not point out the strong probability that whoever killed Major Dakin also killed Leech. And now—Ruth Reddington."

"The man lies," said Dyke, then, scarcely moving his lips.

Friker said, "I believe, Mr. Sanderson, I must arrest you for murder!"

There was another little pause. Behind them the door opened quietly and Elizabeth knew that someone—Charlie and Charmian—had entered the room. Then Dyke laughed shortly.

"Oh, no," he said. "You can't arrest me. I have an alibi. In fact, I have two alibis. I don't know anything about Leech. But I was with Charlie Hawes at the time Uncle Bob was killed. And I was with Charlie just now when we heard the shot." He glanced quickly toward the door, smiled and said, "Tell them, Charlie. Isn't that right?" His glance swept over Elizabeth and Cyril and back to the inspector; he said, "If you don't believe me, search me. You'll find that I don't have the emeralds; I don't have the monkeys— there's nothing . . ." He held up his arms. His coat fell a little open showing a folded paper in his inside coat pocket. The inspector gave him a queer look; and then approached him, as if to take him at his word and search. It was as Friker's hand paused at that paper in his coat pocket that Elizabeth remembered her letter.

26

CHARLIE HAWES, face as white as a sheet, came forward; his hands were working, his eyes bright with fear. He said, "My God, this is terrible. Horrible. Ruth murdered, too. Leech. It's devilish—it's . . ."

The inspector touched Elizabeth's letter; she could see the gray edge of note paper. And Dyke made a sudden and obvious move backward. But for that the inspector might not have taken out the letter. But he did so then, quickly, paying no attention to Charlie.

He opened it. The faintest shadow of a satisfied smile touched Dyke's lips. There was a kind of horror in Elizabeth's heart as she saw it.

And Dyke said, "Tell them, Charlie, what we were doing when we heard the shot in the ravine."

Charlie moistened his lips. The inspector's vivid face was as clear and hard as a diamond as he read Elizabeth's letter.

Charlie said, "That's true. Dyke and I were standing in the doorway, smoking and talking about the fog. We heard the shot and—and we didn't know where it came from—whether from the house or the grounds or what; we started to look. Flemming heard it, too, and came running. Two policemen came running from the back of the house and one from the driveway. Somebody went to telephone—but that's right, Friker; Dyke didn't do it. He couldn't have done it."

Cyril was watching the inspector intently; he turned, caught Elizabeth's eyes and lifted his eyebrows a little. "Is that the letter—" he said so low she thought no one else could have heard.

She nodded hopelessly. Friker, his face completely without expression, finished reading the letter, looked at it thoughtfully for a moment and went to a chair at the long table and sat down, holding the letter in one hand.

"Mrs. Dakin," he said, "I suppose you know what I have here."

Cyril quietly moved away from her; she was aware of that. She was aware, too, of Charmian coming to a chair near by; she had put on a black tea-gown, long, flowing, a little theatrical as always with Charmian. She sat down, her green eyes fastened upon the inspector, the soft chiffon folds falling gracefully around her.

And Elizabeth said huskily, "Yes. I—I know."

"And I suppose you know it establishes the thing we need, and that is a hard and fast motive. A threat. You'd better know that yesterday your chauffeur told me of a quarrel he overheard between you and your husband the night before Major Dakin was murdered. He said among other things that your husband threatened to strangle you before he would let you go to Sanderson. The man to whom you admit you wrote this letter."

"There—there is no threat in my letter. None was intended . . ."

"You said you would do anything to end your marriage; no matter what that meant when you wrote it, it now has only one interpretation. I made a mistake in discounting the chauffeur's story; he said the quarrel was over Sanderson and I—it had seemed to me," said the inspector, "that you were not in love with Sanderson, but with another man. Consequently I did not give the chauffeur's story the weight that I see now it deserved."

Queer, thought Elizabeth, that you had no feeling at all at a time when you ought to feel the most. Was it resignation to catastrophe? Was it a feeling that it couldn't be real? That things like this—murder, death on a foggy path, a letter written by her own hand; a trap of her own making—none of this could really happen to oneself?

The inspector looked at Dyke and said in a voice so sharp and brittle that it was curious it carried so much scorn, "I suppose you supplied her with the gun. You arranged the ladder, obviously, simply for a—a red herring. A false clue which you hoped would

259

confuse us. You left the front door open when you came back into the house for the same reason."

Dyke said quickly, handsome head flung back, "To admit anything like that would be to make myself an accessory before the fact. Isn't that true?"

"You don't need to admit it," said Friker. "When I present evidence, that evidence holds in a court of law."

It was just then that Cyril said from the door, "Sorry—but I'll thank you to put your hands up. All of you."

She whirled around. Everyone looked. And Cyril, standing easily before the door, had one hand in his pocket and the other on the latch of the door.

"I was in the army, Friker," he said. "And I still have my service revolver, as you see. I'm not going to hurt anyone. I only want you to listen. Will you do that?"

The inspector, an image of immobility but a thoughtful image, said after a second or two that they would listen. Charmian made a sudden move and Cyril's hand jerked toward her. *"If you please,"* he said. She lifted her shoulders a little and sat back in her chair. Cyril said, "Thank you. You see, Friker, there are several things that I want you to consider. First, no one could have killed Major Dakin who wasn't acquainted with the house, isn't that right?"

"Are you going to listen to . . ." began Dyke, and Friker said, "Quiet, please. Go on, Mr. Kirby. That's right. It has been obvious from the first."

"Does it seem possible to you that such a person would have entered Elizabeth's suite after shooting Major Dakin, knowing that she would be there and thus taking the risk of being seen?"

"No," said the inspector, "unless he expected her protection."

"But if such a person did not expect her protection, he would not take such a risk?"

"Probably not."

"Well, then. Suppose such a person believed that—that Elizabeth would not be there. Suppose such a person believed that the front door would be left open and that Elizabeth would not be in her suite."

"Where would she be?"

"I don't know. Anywhere; out for a walk in the grounds, in another part of the house; anywhere but in her rooms. Suppose the front door was to be left open, Elizabeth to be gone from her rooms. Very well. Suppose the murderer enters Dakin's study, locks the door into the hall; goes to Dakin who, remember, had been drinking heavily, has perhaps a word or two with him, puts down the wooden monkeys or gives them to him, shoots him without warning and then in order to escape, believing the way is clear because that was the arrangement, unlocks the door to Elizabeth's suite, which Dakin has locked, and enters the little passage. At this point Elizabeth in her dressing room, with the door between it and the little passage closed, moves and knocks over a lamp. The sound of the lamp alarms the murderer and lets the murderer know that someone is there and the suite is not empty as he must have believed. The door of the bathroom directly opposite is open; the murderer has barely time to duck into the bathroom just as Elizabeth comes out of the dressing room and enters the study. Then the murderer comes out of the bathroom, leaves the gun behind the books and scrambles down from the balcony, by the trellis."

"Very well," said the inspector imperturbably. "I won't say this is all a new hypothesis. But go on."

"You say Dyke bought the gun?"

"This gentleman says that," said Friker, waving toward the man from Kingston who, more uneasy than ever and with his little eyes riveted upon Cyril's bulging pocket had retired to his corner again. "You mean that two people conspired to kill Major Dakin?"

"It's what you have said," said Cyril.

"And the other person—besides Dyke Sanderson."

"The other one," said Cyril, "is Charmian. The first Mrs. Dakin."

Charmian sprang up then, her eyes like jewels. "How dare you—I, murder him! That's mad . . . How dare you!"

"Sit down, Mrs. Dakin," said Friker. He rose and walked in a leisurely way toward Cyril. "You can take your hand out of your pocket, you know," he said. "You have no gun there. I let you talk because I wanted to hear it. But you can trust me to see that no one gets away. You think then that Charmian Dakin entered this house through the front door, left

262

open by Dyke Sanderson, shot her former husband and escaped as you have said. Why?"

"For one reason; because I went to her house this afternoon; I inquired; it took a long time but I finally got it out of one of her servants that Ruth had come to see her and that Dyke Sanderson had come to see her. Both of them hours before they first admitted to being in Montego Bay; each obviously without knowledge of the other's visit."

"Even if that were true," said Charmian, "it doesn't have anything to do with Robert's murder. I lost everything by his death. And I knew I was to lose it. I lost twenty-five thousand dollars a year. I knew he would not provide for me in his will, and he didn't. What was my motive, then? Revenge?" She laughed. "What for? We had been divorced for a long time. I had no motive for revenge. All this is sheer nonsense, there is no word of proof. You can't accuse me."

"Why did you come here?" said Cyril.

"Why?" Charmian's eyelids drooped. "I came for exactly the reason I told you. Except I—also—hoped to persuade Elizabeth to give me the emeralds. As she did. That's all. I assure you I wouldn't be such a fool as to kill a man in the faint hope of persuading his wife to give me some jewels."

The inspector said softly: "Well, Mr. Kirby? Is that all? It's an interesting theory. But I have to have proof, you know. To convince a jury."

But Ruth had known. Ruth had known the whole story. Elizabeth started forward. "Ruth knew," she said. "She found the monkeys. She told me. She had the emeralds and the monkeys and she said she took the monkeys from—from Dyke's room, last night."

The inspector looked at Dyke. "You had the monkeys, then? Why did you take them away?"

Dyke's handsome face was sullen. "I didn't. Ruth lied."

"I saw them. She was going to tell me—she did tell me why she came to see Charmian. She wanted to persuade her to—to have my marriage set aside. So Charmian's marriage to Robert would be reinstated. It—oh, it's true. I'll tell you—but there was also an envelope. Ruth gave it to me and asked me to give it to Charlie to put in the safe. And I did. And when I came back Ruth was gone . . ." She stopped, abruptly aware of the complete, utter silence in the room. They were all staring at her. Cyril was the first to move or speak.

"Charlie, where is the envelope? Give it to us—hurry!"

Charlie didn't speak for a moment; his face was like chalk, his little mouth trembled, his eyes darted here and there. And then all at once he began to wring his hands together and shout:

"I don't know anything about it! I tell you I don't know anything about any of this. I—I'm only a bystander. It's nothing to me, any of it. You keep asking me questions; you keep trying to drag me into it. The first thing I know you'll twist it around so it looks as if I killed him. And Leech—and her—it's murder—

264

everywhere. I tell you I don't know anything. I'm out of it. You"—he took a sobbing breath and whirled around to the inspector—"you keep asking me about the filing cabinet where the gun was kept. And it'll be that gun—you mark my words. They'll find it in the ravine and it'll be the gun that was in the cabinet. And I tell you I don't know anything about it. Maybe there were two keys in the beginning, years ago when the cabinet was bought. I only know I had a key and for years it's been the only one. I don't know anything about an envelope Ruth gave anybody. Let me alone, I tell you—*let me alone . . .*" his voice rose to a squeal and broke into sobs and he just stood there, wringing his hands, and trembling, and darting strange, terrified glances at the inspector and Charmian and Dyke and all of them.

27

HE WAS afraid—and as always with Charlie, he was taking refuge in lies. Elizabeth said to Friker: "I can prove it to you. The letter is in the safe. Unless"—a chill thought struck her—"unless he removed it. No one else knows how to open the safe."

"No—no," cried Charlie shrilly. "I didn't . . ."

"Did you remove the letter?" demanded the inspector.

"But I tell you . . ."

"Don't lie. There was a letter. Wasn't there?"

"I—I . . ."

"Wasn't there?"

"Yes," said Charlie sulkily, his shrill defiance collapsing.

"Mrs. Dakin, will you go and get the letter? Hawes will go with you." The inspector paused and added, "Since Hawes did not remove the letter, it must be still in the safe; I want that letter. Understand?"

She did understand; she was to have no opportunity to read and, perhaps—if she had been guilty; if the letter involved her—destroy it.

Cyril started forward. "I'll go, too."

"Sorry," said Friker. "You'll stay here, please, Kirby. And so will everyone else. Except Hawes."

Charlie gave her a sulky look but moved to accompany her. Cyril opened the door for her; there was, in spite of what the inspector had said, a queer kind of warning in his look as if he said, "Look out!"

The hall was empty; they went silently, Charlie still sulky, up the stairway. There was a small light at the end of the corridor above. No one moved along its whole length. They turned, Elizabeth ahead and Charlie following, and went to the study. Charlie turned on the light. No one was in the study either. But everyone else was in the library and Friker would keep them there until she returned.

It was perfectly safe.

There was no sound anywhere except Charlie's nervous fingers on the dials of the safe. But if there had been talking, or even quite loud sounds in the library, they couldn't have heard them at that distance.

Charlie's head was bent over the dials of the safe and she went to stand beside him, so as to be able to see over his shoulder into the safe. And there was a faint little click of the lock and the door swung open. The envelope was exactly where Charlie had placed it. If only the thing inside the envelope proved really

267

to be evidence! The whole story, Ruth had said. But would it be that?

Charlie, staring at the gray envelope suspiciously as if it had been, itself, some kind of lethal instrument, made no effort to take it. And he made no objection when, quickly, she reached for it.

She took it to the light, weighing it in her hand. She knew that Charlie had closed the safe again; she knew he was watching her uneasily. But she was going to read the letter—quickly—then. She must know. She tore the flap and Charlie cried, "No! Don't! You'll get into trouble . . ."

She pulled out closely written, thin gray sheets.

"Mrs. Dakin—you mustn't—I can't be a party to this. I—oh, I wish I was out of this. I . . ." He gave her a despairing glance in which there was a kind of desperate resolve. "I'm going to pack my things! I'm going to leave! Murder—they can't keep me here! I've done nothing. I'm going . . ." He made a queer gesture as if washing his hands of her, of the letter, of everything and scuttled, but very quietly, away.

Elizabeth was scarcely aware of his departure, for she had begun to read.

Ruth's handwriting was clear and businesslike; so, in an odd way were her statements; it was between the lines, for Ruth was not imaginative, that the pictures she suggested took on their true color.

The letter began: "This is to be read in case of my death."

In case of her death.

268

Elizabeth's eyes plunged along the rest of the closely written lines. She read as rapidly as she could, leaping along whole phrases, knowing if she were delayed too long Friker would send for her.

"This is to be read in case of my death. I have told Dyke that I am writing it only in order to protect myself.

"I have made an agreement with him; I will not go to the police with what I know, if he will see that I am safe. I have no proof for the police; but that isn't the reason I don't want to tell them what I know. It's because of Dyke and the horrors of a trial. I can't turn him over to the inspector even though I know the truth. Besides, what's done is done; I had my own part in it and thus part of the blame is mine. Nothing would bring Robert back. And nothing more matters. This statement is written only to insure my safety.

"First, I came to Montego Bay alone and because I wanted to talk to Charmian without anyone knowing it. I saw no reason to tell Dyke about this. And I saw no reason to tell the truth to the inspector when (having told him that Dyke and I made the trip from Texas here together) he thought I meant the entire trip including the motor trip from Kingston to Montego Bay.

"For reasons of my own, I wished to persuade Charmian to enter a plea to have her divorce from Robert Dakin set aside; this could be done; I have in my possession (at home in my office safe) evidence of collusion in securing that divorce. I also had discovered a means to persuade Charmian; a quantity of money might have been, under Texas law, rightfully hers, had she secured her divorce in Texas where she would have had her share

269

of Robert's money. Since the whole divorce suit is ended, she cannot enter suit for that money now; or, if so, would stand every chance of losing it, or so my lawyer informs me. But if her marriage were reinstated she could then later (if she desired) sue again for divorce and this time in Texas where her lawyer could put in a claim for a share of all the money earned by her husband during the years when she was his wife. Robert was several times a millionaire, so it would in all probability have meant a very large lump sum in Charmian's pocket. As to the present Mrs. Dakin, it seemed to my lawyer that an amicable arrangement could have been brought about there, but that did not concern me. I went to see Charmian; she was angry when I told her about the money and she wanted it, but she did not fall in with my plan. She was furious with Robert, too, for having made no offer to divide their money. He must have known what the law was but kept quiet about it, naturally preferring to give her even a large alimony rather than a half or a third of his fortune. I left her at last and she had promised to think it over but I could see that she did not want to be Robert's wife again under any circumstances.

"I went then to the hotel and rested, intending to have dinner and then take a cab to the villa; there was no particular reason for this except it would bear out my excuse to Dyke that I intended to shop in Kingston and thus would make the drive to Montego Bay alone, when I was ready. While I was there Dyke came; I thought he had just then arrived and gave him to understand that I had been there only a short time. We then had dinner together. It did not occur to me then that he might also have arrived earlier than he pretended.

270

"Now I know that he did, and I know about the monkeys.

"They belonged to Robert—I mean the boy. Robert's and Charmian's son. We called him Bobbie. He'd had them since he was a small child and, when he was older, carried them as a luck piece in his pocket. And I remembered after a while that Charmian had taken the monkeys when the boy died.

"I think I'd better try to explain Charmian; I know her so well—or thought I did. I see now where I made my mistake. She was always very intense about everything; violent and emotional; I suppose you'd call it temperamental. I always thought it was as if she played to an audience. She wasn't a loving or good mother; she's too selfish and erratic for that. I used to feel sorry for the boy. But she was proud of the boy; and she seemed to be heartbroken when he died. Perhaps she realized then what she had lost. Her grief wasn't pretense, although so much of Charmian is pretense, it's difficult to know what is real.

"The boy was drowned. I was there; it happened at the summer camp where we—Charmian and Bob, Dyke, the boy and I used to go. Everybody said it was an accident and I thought so, too.

"But I know now that Dyke Sanderson murdered him. I saw him do it.

"It was very simple. I'd better tell about this, too. We were out on the raft, Dyke, the boy, Bob and I. The boy was learning to dive; he went down and Dyke went with him at the same time. Neither came up for a moment, and then Dyke came up at the other side of the raft and asked if the boy had come up. I said, no. I went

271

in for the boy and so did Dyke and Bob. Bob had been drinking a lot that day. Dyke dived and dived and wouldn't give up. It was two hours before we found him and when he was found he had had a blow on the side of his head. Everybody thought he struck the raft accidentally. I thought that Dyke, diving as he did at the same time the boy dived, had accidentally thrust the boy against the raft. He seemed to feel so badly about it that I didn't say anything, for I thought then that it was an accident and it would only cause more grief if I told that it was Dyke's fault. Now I know it was done purposely because Dyke was jealous of the boy and wanted to be Robert's heir. A hundred small things led me to this conclusion.

"This morning, realizing why the monkeys were on the desk (that is, that Charmian in one of her dramatic gestures had shown them to Robert to remind him, before she shot him, and then forgotten to take them away, and that Dyke had realized it, too, and was trying to protect her), I went to Dyke's room and told him that I knew the truth. I guessed what he had told Charmian.

"I don't know how this could be proved except that the monkeys show Charmian was there in the room. I know she kept them always, and I think someone else, Leech, perhaps, could prove this, too.

"But Charmian killed him. Because I had told her of the money that ought to have come to her (she will try to sue for it now that he's dead and cannot defend the suit as he would have done—and successfully—if she had attempted a suit during his lifetime). It was a short cut I didn't see (and if I had seen it, I would never have thought that Charmian would actually think of mur-

272

der). And also because, within an hour of my visit to her, Dyke told her that Robert was drunk (as he was) the afternoon the boy drowned. So drunk that he got into one of his crazy drunken rages and knocked the boy off the raft and was responsible for the boy's death. I think it gave Charmian the frenzy of hatred, and desire for revenge necessary to commit murder; she was always emotional, and Dyke knew it. Or perhaps it justified her actions to herself.

"I told Dyke this; he admitted it and pointed out that he had an alibi. That shows he knew what she was going to do. I think he gave her the gun, told her the front door would be left open, and promised perhaps to see that Elizabeth was not in her suite. Robert's locking up Elizabeth spoiled that part of the plan.

"But Charmian wouldn't have done it if she hadn't known about the money. Not Charmian.

"Dyke suggested murder; he wanted Bob's money. He told her Bob was responsible for the boy's death to rouse her; he didn't know that what he really did was suggest to Charmian a short cut to all that money.

"If anything happens to me, I don't know how you can prove this or whether it will be admissible in court. But it will show you where to look.

"I think he has told Charmian that I know. This is all. You can compare my signature here with other signatures to prove it is genuine."

It was signed Ruth Reddington.

Elizabeth leaned back against the desk, staring downward at her wet, muddy pumps. Proof?

But what about the emeralds? Ruth had had the

emeralds and the monkeys. If Charmian had forced her to go to the ravine (and Charmian had had the gun; she must have had it—hidden perhaps in her knitting bag after—why, after Friker himself had seen it was empty!) then Ruth had taken the emeralds and the monkeys with her. There had been a moment or two, longer perhaps, between the time when she heard the shot and the time she had come out upon the path and found Ruth. Plenty of time for Charmian to take the emeralds and the monkeys. And after Elizabeth herself escaped Charmian, and Cyril and the police came, there'd been time, too, for Charmian to evade the policemen and Cyril and herself in the dusk and in the fog and return to the house; if Dyke saw her it would not matter, for he had known.

She saw suddenly that Dyke must have known at least part of what Charmian intended to do in the distant, fog-masked ravine. He had known about the letter; Ruth had told him. Had he told Charmian? Almost certainly he had told her as much as he dared. Withholding what Ruth knew of his own guilt; frightened, perhaps—yet hoping that Charmian would save herself and him.

Rather horribly, but very clearly, a little dialogue suggested itself to her:

"I'll see to Ruth." That was Charmian.

"No—not murder again—it's dangerous." Dyke would have been reluctant.

"Leave it to me."

"What are you going to do?" (He would have been

274

uneasy here; frightened almost as much of Charmian as of Ruth.)

"Never mind. Elizabeth knows, too; I'm sure of it. Ruth's talking to her now."

"Elizabeth! Look here, Charmian . . ."

"Oh, I know you want her money. Well—" (she must have thought rapidly here; and then lied). "Nothing will happen to the girl. I promise you. It's only Ruth—I'll see to it. But you've got to help me."

He would have been uneasy there, too. "Help you?"

Perhaps Charmian had laughed. And had said, "Bring Elizabeth to the ravine. Right away. Lose her there—anyhow; then get back to the house quickly, if you know what's good for you."

"Charmian—what are you going to do?"

"Never mind. It's best for you not to know. But remember; we are in this together. Do as I tell you. Quickly."

Had their eyes met, sharing a fearful knowledge? Yet Dyke's eyes would have been evasive, pretending not to know.

She moved uneasily, as if to escape the scene her own thoughts had conjured up. Yet—something like that must have occurred.

And Dyke—rather desperately, caught in the trap of his own making, afraid of Charmian, afraid of exposure—had taken Elizabeth to the ravine, and then hurried back to the house to establish an alibi for himself.

Charmian was ahead of them in the ravine; she succeeded with part of her plan. She almost succeeded with the rest of it. Would have succeeded, perhaps, had it not been for the fog. And when Elizabeth escaped her and Cyril came, Charmian had stolen back to the house through the concealing fog. There was time, too, for Charmian to hurry to her room, change her dress and—and of course, her sodden slippers, and then come downstairs. The actress, playing a role; dramatic in her black, trailing gown. Daring because she had so little, now, to lose.

But the emeralds and the monkeys and the muddy slippers must be in Charmian's room somewhere.

It was still quiet; no one was anywhere about. She'd better find the emeralds and the monkeys and take them, as proof, along with Ruth's letter.

She went out of the study and along the deserted hall and into the corner guest room Charmian was using. She closed the door and turned on the light. Charmian's things were everywhere. A negligee over one chair, a pale green dress flung over another; towels and stockings in a heap on the floor; dressing table laden and untidy with powder spilled and lipstick tube open and a small pair of scissors, sharp and shining, on the floor.

In the mirror she caught a glimpse of her own face, pale and streaked with dirt, her hair wet and curling and wildly disheveled where leaves had caught it.

There were no emeralds and no little wooden monkeys.

She glanced around the room. There were a hundred places to hide the emeralds and the monkeys. It would be better after all for the police to search them out. But the shoes Charmian must have worn in the ravine—where were they?

She went to the large clothes closet. And just as she reached the door there were two revolver shots from somewhere below. Loud, crashing in waves, reverberating through the house. She stopped, frozen. And, as if a door had swung open there came a kind of wave of voices, shouts, thuds, another shot, louder this time, a sound as if a table had gone over with a tremendous crash, and then it was as if the door closed again, shutting off those sounds.

And just then she saw the slippers Charmian had worn in the ravine. Muddy, still wet, covered with leaf mold—black, high-heeled slippers thrust in a corner of the closet behind the trailing green folds of a dinner gown.

She had to have them; she went into the closet and thrust back the dress and fumbled for the slippers and turned. And the door closed behind her, shutting off all sound and all light. She heard the key on the outside turn, with a clear little click.

She tried to scream and couldn't. What had she done with Ruth's letter? But it was clutched in her hand, tight. What was happening downstairs—who was outside that door? Why?

She put her hand on the doorknob and it turned under her hand, and Charmian said, low, on the other side of the door, "Give me the letter and I'll let you go. Give me the letter Ruth wrote." She paused and then said, low and hoarsely, "Nobody will come, you know. Dyke said something Kirby didn't like; before anybody could stop them they were fighting. Friker shot several times in the air. I turned off the lights and got away; they won't know it until too late. Unless you—Listen, Elizabeth. After one murder, others are easy. Slide the letter under the door."

The voice trailed away in the distance. There was no sound at all for a moment. Then there was a soft rustle again, and it spoke quite clearly, against the door. "It's my life or yours. I promised Dyke I wouldn't hurt you—he needs your money, you know. I told him to bring you to the ravine; and to ask no questions. He had to do it; he was too deeply involved to dare to refuse. But he's a coward; he didn't want to know what I—what I had to do. Do you understand? I had to kill Ruth and I did. But if you'll give me the letter I'll—I'll let you off. The letter is the only proof—nobody would believe you. I promise you I'll . . ." She took a short, hard breath. "Robert must have told you; Ruth told you what she knew . . . You've been waiting to trap me. Well, I've got something here—hurry, slide the letter under the door . . ."

There was an abrupt silence. Then she heard Charmian's voice again. *"You . . ."* she said.

A chair crashed over. Someone shouted not far away. People were running. Something else crashed.

278

There were shouts, footsteps—and all at once silence. Elizabeth tried to scream again and thrust herself against the door and pulled at the knob.

And Cyril opened it. He caught her in his arms and just held her, tight, for a long time before he said, his mouth against her face, "It's all right, Elizabeth. It's all over."

She only clung to him.

They were standing like that, locked in each other's arms when Friker came into the room. His hair was ruffled, his tie awry, and he had Elizabeth's letter in his hand. He gave them one brilliant glance.

"Take this," he said, and thrust the letter into Elizabeth's hand. "I'd advise you to destroy it." He saw the other envelope, Ruth's, and added, "And I'll take that. Sanderson's down there talking as hard and fast as he can. Swears he only took you"—he nodded to Elizabeth—"to the ravine because Charmian insisted. Says he didn't know what she was going to do; says he didn't know Ruth was there or Charmian either, and that Charmian promised you were safe. Not very consistent. He's an accessory all right; has been from the first. We're going to search the room; the emeralds must be here and the monkeys and the clothes she wore in the ravine . . ."

"Slippers," said Elizabeth and was a little surprised when her voice came out as a thin whisper. She pointed. "In there . . ."

Friker, his hand on the closet door, turned and shot

one hard bright look at Cyril. "How did you guess in the first place?"

"Oh, that. Dakin told Elizabeth, before he died."

"Told *me*? But he didn't . . ."

"Yes, he did. He said 'Elizabeth shot me. Help.' Then later he said, 'Charmian, don't go.' After a while, at the last, he opened his eyes and said, addressing you, Elizabeth, 'Charmian, no, I mean Elizabeth.' He often confused your names, especially when he was drinking. What I think he actually meant to say was 'Charmian shot me' and then, 'Elizabeth, don't go.' "

"That made you suspect Charmian?" said Friker.

"Only suspect."

"She had the second key to the filing cabinet," said the inspector. "It was bought while she lived here; she must have had it and have known about the revolver. She forgot the monkeys—and she knew Leech would remember . . ." He stopped suddenly, and unexpectedly smiled.

It was the first time she had ever seen him smile. It was like a metamorphosis. Like sun on a stormy day. He said with a little bow, "You have things to say to each other; I'll leave you alone. But I do want to say, Mr. Kirby, that difficult as it made things for me at the moment, I did enjoy the beautiful punch you gave Sanderson. Right to the jaw." He bowed again and went away, the slippers and the letter in his hand.

Cyril said, "Look here, Elizabeth. I—disowned you last night because I wanted to get hold of the letter

Dyke had before I told him the truth. About you, I mean; that I love you and intend to marry you. Give it to me."

He took the letter from her; he lighted a match and touched it to the letter and she reached for an ashtray and held it under the flames. They watched it in silence as it turned brown and crisp and fell into the ashtray.

Cyril took the tray away from her and said, "That's an end to that. Forever. Now listen, Elizabeth. There'll be time for talk later. All I want to say now is this. I heard this noon; there's a boat tomorrow. I've got to take it. Elizabeth—the world is wide. And war changes things. So the real things—love and time—are so terribly important. Elizabeth, I want you . . ."

But he stopped then and took her in his arms.

It didn't matter about the world being wide. She wanted it only as wide as the circumference of his arms. War. She would not think of that, then. She moved closer within his arms.

He put back her head and said, "My, but your face is dirty. The ravine . . ." His own face sobered. He held her tighter, and then bent to her lips.